DEDICATION

This, the last book
in the Freedom Series,
is lovingly dedicated to
four wonderful young adults:
Sonya Renee, our daughter,
and
Kyer Toney, our son,
and
Pamela Kay Phillips, our daughter-in-law,
and
Matthew Ray Hinchman, our son-in-law.

Lo, children are an heritage of the Lord.
Psalm 127:3

I love you all.
Mom

PREFACE

We first met Will and Hannah in the year 1752 in Germany. *Freedom in White Mittens* tells the story of how they came to America in search of freedom from the tyranny of riches in their homeland.

Freedom's Destiny Fulfilled moved the story ahead fourteen years. In this book, we met the Stivers' children: Freedom Duffy, Liberty Lucille and William Justice. The family moved via covered wagon from Norfolk, Virginia, to Ohio. Duffy went off to fight for freedom and was killed at Point Pleasant, the battle that many believe was the first battle of the American Revolution. His destiny was fulfilled but the saga of the rest of the family continues.

As *Freedom's Tremendous Cost* begins, the year is 1820. Will has recently gone to be with the Lord. Hannah is eighty-five years old and is about to begin a new quest for freedom. Libby is sixty-two years old. She and Sam have a large dairy farm at Kelly's Creek. Libby's daughter, Dilly, is forty-six years old. She is married to Frank, lives at Burning Springs, and is busy with her three children. Willy is now fifty years old. He has built himself a house just up the hill from where his parents lived. He remained a bachelor until later in life, but is now happy and content with his wife of several years, Nancy.

In 1790, thirteen years before Ohio became a state, five hundred French people followed the Ohio River in search of freedom from the horrors of the revolution in their country. They began to build houses just a few miles east of the Stivers' home. Thus the town of

Gallipolis was born.

Come back with me to 1820 and learn once again of Will and Hannah's dream of freedom. Enjoy.

Raelene Phillips

The family tree is as follows:

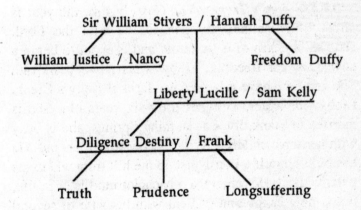

Chapter One

True waited impatiently in the springboard wagon.

"Prudy, what's taking them so long?" she asked her younger sister. "If we don't get going soon, the day will be half spent."

"Mayhap Cowma is going along after all," Prudy replied. "Yes, that seems to be it. See, Mama and Grandma are helping her down the steps. Best we drive the wagon up to the mounting block," she added as she sprawled up into the tail of the wagon in a very unladylike manner.

"Hang on then," True shot back over her shoulder as she gave the horses a flick of the reins. "And Prudence," she continued in her best schoolmarm voice, "It is high time you quit referring to Great-Grandma Hannah as 'Cowma.' It was all right when you were a toddler. Rather endearing actually. But now you're a grown-up girl of ten. It's time to . . ."

Never one to cower to her sister who was eight years her senior, Prudy tossed her red-gold curls as she interrupted, "I don't have to obey you. Mama says that just 'cause you're my teacher during school, I don't has ta listen to ya and do yer biddin' all summer vacation. 'Sides, Cowma doesn't mind me calling her that. Do ya, Cowma?"

By now the trio of ladies, all dressed in stylish black for their shopping spree in town, had made their way down the twelve steps from the porch and the long, marigold-lined sidewalk to the hitching post and mounting block at the road.

For a few minutes all energy and attention were focused on helping eighty-five-year-old Hannah Stivers step over the side of the wagon and settle herself comfortably on the high-backed seat.

"Lands, I can't believe it's such a chore just to get in a wagon," Hannah puffed. "Why, it just seems like yesterday my Will and I were walking through Germany, and now I get plum tuckered after jist walkin' out here to River Road."

"Are you comfortable, Mama?" asked Libby. "Is your leg paining you much today?" she inquired as she arranged a quilt over the old lady's stiff right leg which had been placed out and over the tongue-board of the spring wagon.

"You don't care if I call you Cowma, do you?" persisted the freckle-faced child with the strawberry-blonde ringlets.

"Land sakes, Prudy, hush! We're trying to determine if Grandma is comfortable here!" Dilly glared at her youngest as she spoke.

"But Mama, True said I should quit calling her Cowma! Do I has ta?"

"Have to," corrected the perturbed True. "I don't think you learned anything about proper grammar in school last term."

"True! Prudy! Honestly! Can't you stop your bick-

ering for once? Go ahead, True. I think we're settled,"
Dilly clucked as she plopped down on the quilts beside
Prudy. Libby had seated herself on the outside of the
seat with a protective arm around Hannah's shoulders.

"What's the quibbling all about?" Hannah asked
with a twinkle in her eye as she glanced over her
shoulder at her youngest great-granddaughter.

"True says that I should quit calling you Cowma
now that I'm growed up."

"Grown!" sighed True.

The white-haired Hannah turned her gaze on Libby
and Sam's eldest granddaughter. "Oh, True, don't take
on so. I've always thought it was sweet the way Prudy
combined the name of her favorite animal with
Grandma and Grandpa and invented her own special
names for Will and me. Wouldn't hardly sound right
for her to call me anything else. And I know her Cowpa
loved it when she . . ." Hannah's voice broke and she
reached in her reticule for a clean handkerchief.

"It's okay, Grandma," said Dilly as they all tried to
forget the recent tragedy.

"Okay, ladies, what are we going to buy in Gallipolis today?" As usual, Dilly got everyone to put aside
their somber thoughts and focus on the business at
hand. Already they could see the outermost homes of
the burgeoning town ahead.

"I need to find some calico piece goods. I've got an
idea for new curtains and a tablecloth to match for the
teachery," exclaimed True. "I never can remember the
way to figure for nice full curtains. Mama, do I want
two or three times the width of the window?"

Dilly looked at her mother inquiringly. "They hang

prettiest iffen you triple the window, don't they, Mama?'' In truth, Dilly knew the answer but had realized long ago that Libby needed to be needed. Since Dilly was the only child Libby and Sam had been able to raise to adulthood, she felt somewhat responsible to keep them happy.

"At least three times the window width, True," replied Libby. "What color are ya aimin' for?"

"Blue, I think, or maybe green. What about you, Mama? Are you looking for anything special today? We're almost there."

The cabins of the original French five hundred lined the road on either side. Up ahead a few blocks one could see the huge sign of the recently opened Le Clerque Mercantile.

Dilly stated matter-of-factly, "My only purchase shall be a paper of pins. I don't know how I lose so many but after each dress is completed, it seems I'm short twenty or more pins." Since moving up-river to the settlement of Burning Springs with her husband and family, Dilly was in constant demand as a dressmaker.

"What about you, Cowma?" asked Prudy as the wagon came to a full stop and True hitched the horses to the post in front of the store. "Did you just come along for the ride, or are you coming in to buy something too?"

"I've given my money to Libby. I want some fine white wool to knit a sweater for Willy's baby. Since it's a-goin' to be a winter baby, it'll need a nice heavy sweater. But you best go in with the others, Prudy. Tell your Grandma that she is to buy some horehound drops for you and yer brother out of my money. Whilst you all are in there shopping, I'll just rest my eyes a spell."

"Thank you, Cowma!" Prudy bounced into the store shouting, "Grandma!" as she went.

Hannah smiled as she leaned back on the crude seat covered with an old quilt and closed her eyes. Prudy looked so much like Libby except for her hair which undoubtedly came from Sam's side of the family. The Kellys were red-headed Irishmen through and through.

"Hello, Mrs. Stivers. Good to see you out and about on such a fine autumn day. What brings you into town?"

It was the parson who had spoken so eloquently at Will's funeral just two weeks ago.

"Good afternoon, Parson Swank. Yes, it is a lovely day. The girls all insisted that I needed to get out. I hope folks won't think it unseemly of me. But they are all fixing to leave for home a few days hence. Libby needs to get back to Sam and the cows at their farm on Kelly's Creek. And Dilly has women waitin' fer her to make dresses fer them. Can't believe it's nigh time fer school to begin. Did you know True teaches at the school at Burning Springs?"

"I can't quite keep up with your family, Ma'am," the reverend blushed. "Are you sayin' there's four generations of Stivers women on this venture into town today?"

"Why, yes" Hannah chuckled. "Though I never thought on it, I guess there are. Me, I'm the oldest - then there's my daughter, Libby - then her daughter, Dilly - then her two daughters, True and Prudy. That makes four generations, sure enough."

"Wouldn't Will be proud to see all his ladies together?" The minister gave Hannah a rueful smile.

"Yes, mayhap he would." The old lady's eyes grew bright. "I never got me an opportunity to thank you, Parson Swank, for yer message that day. It was just what my Will would have wanted."

"He'll certainly be missed, Ma'am. But, iffen yer family is all about to go home as you said, what do you plan to do?"

"Why, I just plan to go on as best I kin, Parson. Willy and his sweet wife have insisted that I move in with them. Ya know, she's in the family way and they'll be needin' some help when the next Stivers is born in a few months. The girls have all helped to fetch and carry my things up the hill to Will's house. So, fer now, I'll be stayin' with them. Iffen this bum leg of mine gets to bendin' a little better come spring, I'm aimin' to move back down the hill to Will's and my cottage. I'd rather be in my own place, but I don't want to be a bother to the children either."

"Your Willy is a good man, Mrs. Stivers. I was there in the sickroom with him when he promised his Pa he'd take care of you. That seemed to relieve Will's mind so much. It was shortly after that when he left us."

Hannah nodded. "As much as I miss him, I wouldn't wish him back to this life, Brother Swank. Mayhap some day doctors will know how to care for folks who get the sickness my Will had. Seemed like he just went down and down. Once he lost his eyesight, though, it was so sad. He'd try to get up and he'd bump into the wall and . . .''

"Don't relive it, Ma'am," the parson instructed.

"He's in a much better place now. And he's whole!"

"Cowma, they're comin'. Do you want a piece of my candy?"

"Yours and Long's, you mean," Hannah corrected as she reached into the sack of horehound. "Say hello to the minister and offer him a piece of your candy."

The little girl obeyed, but the preacher refused.

"Your family's names never cease to amaze me," he smiled, glancing over his shoulder to see if the other shoppers were coming.

"We chose to name our children Freedom, Liberty, and Justice because those three things were so important to us. Will and I were surprised when Libby continued the tradition by naming her daughter Diligence. And, oh my, we were so thrilled and pleased when Dilly and Frank continued the family tradition by giving us Truth and then the twins, Longsuffering and Prudence."

"If they all live up to their names, they shall have achieved a lot," Rev. Swank retorted. "Ah, here come the rest of Will's ladies now. I must be on my way also. We are anxious to have you back in services, Mrs. Stivers."

"As soon as this rheumatiz in my leg lessens some. Stop on out to see us sometime, Brother Swank."

As the two ended their conversation, the shoppers all climbed up into the wagon chattering merrily.

"See the yarn, Mama," Libby said. "Isn't it fine? Doesn't it remind you . . .?"

"'Twas so long ago, Lib. I'm plum surprised you remember."

"Oh, Mama, how could I forget? Prudy, you come

up here and sit quietly. Mama is going to tell us the story of Papa's mittens that became a sweater and then became a muffler for my brother, your Great-Uncle Duffy.''

''They've heard it before,'' Hannah argued, shaking her head.

''Please, Cowma, please! Start in Germany! Tell me again!''

And so the family listened once again as Hannah began with, ''Back in those days it was high fashion for men to wear mittens.'' And the re-telling of the story proved to be therapy for the grieving heart of Will's lady, Hannah Stivers.

Chapter Two

"We won't call it a farewell dinner, Mama. It's just a dinner," insisted Nancy, Willy's wife. "The girls aren't that far away. Why, it's just down the Kanawha."

"Mayhap you're right. But still and all, we know it'll be a time and a time afore we see each other again." Hannah swiped at the tear that ran down her wrinkled cheek unbidden, glancing around furtively hoping none of the others had seen.

The conversation took place as the last-minute touches were put on the evening meal. Hannah was placing the white linen napkins around the table. Libby gave the potatoes a few final punches with the masher.

"They need a mite more milk, Nancy," she stated as she reached for the bottle. Her sister-in-law, huge with child, was lumbering back and forth from the dry sink to the table with glasses of milk for the children and Willy, who had never acquired a taste for coffee. Dilly was pouring coffee for the ladies, while True rounded up extra chairs. Prudy had been sent to find her twin brother, Long. They, along with Willy, had just finished washing their hands at the pump just off the back stoop when Hannah shouted, "Suppertime! C'mon, everyone.''

As they all gathered at the table and found their seats, they grasped each other's hands automatically. Willy thanked the Lord for the bounteous spread of food before them and then broadened his prayer to remember his missing brother-in-law and nephew.

"Lord, we ask you to watch over Sam and his cows. Keep them safe. We know he'll be right glad to see Libby day after tomorrow. And God, also sustain Frank as he prepares for the return of Dilly and the children tomorrow. Keep the packet boat safe as it journeys down the Kanawha takin' our kin home. Lord, we're gonna miss 'em but we know life's gotta go on. Bless us all for Jesus' sake. Amen.''

"Don't let go hands, please," implored True before Willy even had the Amen fully out of his mouth. "Could we sing the blessing?"

"Oh, yes, let's do!" Hannah agreed.

And so, even though Dilly and her children had Irish blood in their veins and though Nancy was fully English-American, they all joined in perfect German to sing.

> *Gott ist die Liebe, Lasst mich erlosen;*
> *Gott ist die Liebe, er liebt auch mich.*
> *Drum sag ich nocn einmal: Gott ist die Liebe,*
> *Gott ist die Liebe, er liebt auch mich.*

Once they got started in unison, Libby dropped to sing alto and Willy's full bass made it sound like a choir. As the last note sounded, Hannah pulled True over in a tight hug. The tears that always seemed so close to the surface these days flowed freely and her voice cracked as she said, "Thank you, True. Your

Papa, Frank, gave us a wonderful family tradition when he taught us that song all those years ago when you were tiny. It is wonderful to sing about how much God loves us. And it's always a special treat to Will and . . . er, I mean . . . to me, to hear German again. It's a pretty language.''

Flustered and angry at herself for the emotional display at what she wanted to be a happy meal, Hannah looked down. "Why do I keep bringing up his name like that? When will I realize that he's gone?'' she thought.

"When are we gonna eat? Will someone please pass the chicken?'' Long's desperate-sounding voice broke the tense moment. From then on the usual conversation and playful banter flowed freely throughout the meal.

While Nancy cleared the dishes and Dilly served Hannah's contribution to the meal, a deep-dish apple cobbler still warm from the oven, Libby turned her attention to her brother.

"Willy, you're quiet tonight. Somethin' eatin' away at ya?'' she asked.

Willy brushed his hand across his eyes in a movement so reminiscent of his father that Libby caught her breath. With his square jaw and blue-black eyes, Willy resembled Pa so much that sometimes it hurt to look at him.

"No, I'm just a little tired,'' he lied.

"Did somethin' go amiss at yer work today, son?'' Hannah interjected. Willy had been working as a builder in Gallipolis since 1790 when the town was established by the five hundred people who fled to America from the horrors of the French Revolution.

"No," he insisted. "It's just been a long day. Prudy and Long, if you're finished whyn't you go out back and play? There's not much daylight left."

The children were more than glad to obey. Sensing that the grown-ups needed some time alone, True insisted that she would clean up the supper dishes.

"It's time I did something to earn my keep. We've mooched off Great-Uncle Willy and Great-Aunt Nancy for nigh onto three weeks here. All of you go on into the parlor and relax." After a few weak protests, the older generations complied. Hannah picked up her knitting needles. Libby stood at the large front parlor window and stared down at the river.

"No matter what happens, the mighty Ohio flows on. Mama, have you e'er been sorry that you settled out here to the east of the mouth of the Kanawha? Iffen you'd a-gone the same distance west, you'd a-been right in the heart of Gallipolis."

Willy answered for their Mama. "Oh, Lib, you know the answer to that. You know how Pa hated to be bound in by city folk. That's why me and him picked this here land. The hills are just rolling enough that it was a chore to farm. Pa figured no one else would e'er want to move right on top of us here."

Libby and Hannah exchanged a knowing smile. It was hard to keep from reminding Willy that when he and Pa picked their land, Willy had been only five years old. But Willy was continuing.

"Pa wanted to be free from other people. He didn't want no neighbors a-crowdin' him. Freedom was so important to him. He thought everyone had a right to be free." His voice had risen to a deep roar. "And I do too! Everyone should be free! God created us all equal.'' He slammed his hand hard on the chair arm with the last statement.

Nancy's big blue eyes looked like saucers as she stared at her husband, then looked inquiringly at Hannah. What could have caused him to be so upset?

"William Justice, whyn't you just out with whatever's botherin' you?'' his mother asked quietly.

Willy stood and slowly pulled a piece of paper out of his overall pocket. He was red-faced and trembling as he straightened the sheet. "I saw this today. I pulled it off the hitching post in front of the tavern just as you enter town.''

"What is it? Couldn't you get in trouble for doing that?'' asked Dilly as they all gathered near the settee where Hannah and Nancy remained seated.

"They'll never miss it. This flyer is posted on every tree and building in Gallipolis. There were men putting 'em up all over town.''

Hannah read the flyer aloud, slowly and distinctly.

TO BE SOLD AND LET BY PUBLIC AUCTION
ON SATURDAY, OCTOBER 15, 1820
UNDER THE TREES
NEAR THE TOWN CENTER
OF
PHILLIPSBURG, KENTUCKY

▼ ▼ ▼ ▼ ▼

THE FOLLOWING: 33 SLAVES
BOTH MALE AND FEMALE
THE YOUNGEST BEING 10
THE OLDEST BEING 36

ALL IN GOOD HEALTH
SOME GOOD BREEDER STOCK
▲ ▲ ▲ ▲ ▲
SALE TO BEGIN AT 10:00 A.M.

The room was completely silent when Hannah finished.

"I've ne'er seen anything so vile in my life," Libby exclaimed. "Why on earth would they be postin' these signs here in Ohio? Surely they know it is a free state. I don't understand."

"They just want to remind us and keep us constantly aware that even though we don't allow it here, the horrid institution of slavery still exists," Willy replied.

"Surely they don't think anyone in Gallipolis would be interested in slaves," Nancy interjected. "Why, the Frenchmen all came here to be free of the oppression in their own country."

"Don't be so sure," Willy responded. "I saw some men reading that flyer mighty closely. I just wish there was something - anything - we could do."

"Do about what?" Long asked as the twins bounced into the room. "It's gettin' too dark to see out back. 'Sides, the skeeters have nearly et me alive!"

Willy wadded up the hated flyer again and threw it into the fire. All the adults silently agreed that the children should not see such things.

"It's time for you children to get to bed. We've a long trip ahead of us tomorrow," Dilly warned.

"Mayhap we all should go to bed. Suddenly I'm bone weary," Hannah said.

Goodnights were said all around and everyone found

their beds to be a welcome sight. But Willy lay awake long into the night. "There ought to be something we can do," he thought.

At the dock the next morning, there were many tears. Prudy and Long begged Cowma to come visit them for a long spell.

"Mayhap she can come home with us at Christmas time," Dilly quieted the children.

Libby whispered to Willy to please keep in close touch with them via the mail packet.

"If Mama needs me . . ."

"I'll let you know," the brother promised.

In a scene which had become commonplace to the family during the years since Will and Hannah moved into Ohio, three lonely figures stood on shore and waved as the boat rounded the bend from the Ohio to the Kanawha.

"I get so tired of goodbyes," Hannah sighed as she walked up the hill to Willy's house arm-in-arm with Nancy.

Willy's voice caught as he agreed. "I think the best thing about Heaven must be that there won't ever be a reason to say goodbye up there."

"Amen!" responded Nancy and Hannah in unison.

Chapter Three

For the next several days, the skies were gray. The rainfall varied from a light mist to heavy downpours. But inside Willy's lovely home at the top of the rise overlooking the Ohio, all were snug and dry.

One evening as Nancy sat embroidering yet another of the sacques which were to be the new baby's wardrobe, Hannah rose stiffly and rubbed the back of her neck.

"There!" she announced. "It's all done."

And with as much of a flourish as she could muster, she laid the tiny white hooded sweater on the settee between Willy and Nancy.

"May this baby of your'n wear it in good health," she smiled.

"Oh, Mama," exclaimed her daughter-in-law, "It's lovely! I know it's been a labor of love. How can we ever thank you?"

There was a twinkle in Hannah's eyes and her ever-present dimple showed as she replied, "Just hurry up and give me another grandchild. It seems we've been a-waitin' forever on this one."

"Mama," interjected Willy, "It is so good to see you smile again."

"I know, son," Hannah said, sobering. "Sometimes I feel guilty if I think a happy thought. T'other day I caught myself humming as I made up the bed in the morning. And I felt so guilty. Here I haven't been a widow a month. But . . . somehow . . ."

"Mama, don't feel guilty," Willy ordered. "Papa wouldn't want that. Anyways, it seems to me mayhap we did all our mourning months ago when Papa first took sick."

Nancy stared into the sitting-room fire, her eyes bright with unshed tears. "No," she said, "I don't feel real deep sadness over Papa's death any more. He was so helpless and so frustrated these last months. It's hard to really mourn any more. Every time I think of him, I just picture him walking 'round Heaven with no stoop to his back, a-gettin' acquainted with all them people in the Bible . . . you know, like Jonah and Isaiah and Paul and John."

"And gettin' re-acquainted with his mother and our three little babies," Hannah added, smiling. "But it's time for this weary old woman to go to bed. I'm a-hopin' that the sun will shine tomorrow. We've a heap of garden truck to be stowed away for winter. And it'd just be right nice to be able to get outside, too. Goodnight, children."

The old lady wisely tried to give the young couple, soon to become a family, some time alone together each evening. She retired to her room off the kitchen and read her Bible while the young people sat before the fire.

"I only have one regret," Willy mused as he cradled his wife in his arms.

"What's that, love?" Nancy asked as she leaned against him.

"I just wish Pa could've lived long enough to meet this little chap," he chuckled as he playfully patted her protruding stomach.

She took hold of his hand and held it against her abdomen quietly. Suddenly Willy's hand bounced and he drew back in alarm.

"Forevermore, Nancy! Don't that hurt? The little feller sure has strong legs, don't he?"

Nancy smiled and looked down. "Willy, the little feller could be a little lady."

"Oh, I know," Willy mused, "And I'll love it equal no matter what. When do you think it'll get here so's we can know?"

"Well, it should be in the next couple weeks. I'm bone weary of the waitin' and I hope it's soon."

"Be patient, Nancy. Be patient."

Three weeks later Hannah and Nancy were just walking up the hill from Hannah's house. The marigolds along the walkway had bowed their heads in acquiescence to last night's frost. The leaves that were left on the trees were every shade of red, gold and orange. Beyond these the sky was bright blue.

"Let's set a spell on this old log," requested the mother-in-law. She feigned a weariness she did not feel so that the young soon-to-be mother wouldn't realize Hannah's worries about the baby.

Nancy rubbed the small of her back. "We surely did accomplish lots this day, didn't we, Mama? The carrots are all stored in the sand in your root cellar and before nightfall Willy should have all your apples pressed."

"Yes, and I'm especially thankful that we got everything at my place all cleaned and battened-down like afore it gets any colder. I'm a-thinkin' our Indian summer is about nigh over. I hope you haven't overdone yourself today, child."

"No, Mama, it just seems I've been burstin' with energy all day. But I am a might worried about the baby. Seems it's been awfully quiet all day."

"'Tis nothing, Nancy. Just be patient."

The dark-haired Nancy gave her mother-in-law a pathetic imitation of a smile. "'Twixt you and Willy, I'm gettin' mighty tired of those words, *be patient.* Willy even said last night that seeing as how the baby is late in comin', iffen it's a girl mayhap we should name her Patience seeing as how that's what this is all teachin' us. Ooh! This ache in my back is startin' to be more like sharp pains, Hannah."

Hannah smiled. Her daughter-in-law didn't seem to realize that she vacillated between calling her Mama and Hannah.

"Best we git on up to the house," Hannah said guardedly as she gave her heavy daughter-in-law a gentle tug. "It's taking off cold again since the sun went behind that cloud."

Hannah knew all the signs of the onset of childbirth well . . . the burst of energy, the quiet baby, the aching back. "Don't know why something as natural as birthing babies should frighten us mortals so," she mused as she heated water later that evening.

She had to laugh at Willy. He was in and out of the bedroom a hundred times. He kept repeating, "If only there was something I could do." In truth, he was getting on the ladies' nerves.

Nancy had tried joking, "Be patient, Willy, like you're always tellin' me." But Willy just paced like a caged tiger. "If only there . . ."

Hannah interrupted him. "There is, son. There's wood to be chopped. The more you chop now, the less time you will have to spend doin' it and bein' away from this young'n in the future."

Willy jumped at the idea of having something physical to do. As he went out the back door, Nancy smiled.

"Oh, Hannah, you are a God-send. That son of yours was nigh onto driving me insane. He's . . . Oh! Ooh - Hannah!" This last was said through clenched teeth as yet another labor pain washed over her like a mighty wave on the Ohio in a springtime thunderstorm.

Willy never knew how long he chopped wood that night. He went at it like a man possessed. Sweat escaped every pore even though as Hannah had predicted, the weather had "taken off cold." As soon as he had split one log to the size of the stovebox, Willy grabbed another. A sort of rhythm developed and chips flew high above his massive shoulders. With every stroke of his ax, he prayed for his wife. Finally, between the strokes of his ax, he heard a faint cry.

Could it be? Yes, now there was definitely the sharp cry of a newborn piercing the otherwise still night.

He dropped his ax and bounded to the porch in three mighty leaps. Once inside, though, he turned suddenly shaky. What if . . .?

His worries were soon dispelled by a smiling Hannah who proudly opened the bedroom door.

"Come in, William Justice," she said using the

name reserved for special occasions. "Come in and meet your son."

Hannah left her son and his wife alone as she began to brew some coffee. A baby's birth never ceased to confound Hannah. She felt herself trying to hold in tears of joy and relief and longing for Will as the aroma of coffee filled the kitchen. She was just pouring the strong black liquid into cups when Willy burst into the kitchen.

"Mama, come here. We want to know what you think," he pleaded as he took one of the coffee cups.

Nancy was resting against the pillows with the beautiful baby already taking his first meal at her breast. Hannah was pleased to notice that Nancy pulled the blanket over her exposed shoulder as they entered the room, displaying modesty that much of her generation seemed to have abandoned.

"Think about what?" Hannah asked.

"Well, Mama, we've been a-thinkin' and a-thinkin' on a name for this child. Iffen it had been a girl, we were going to name her Patience. But since God saw fit to give us a son, that name won't fit. I've been tryin' to think of a name that would mean something special. You know, like all of our family's names do. E'er since I saw that poster about that slave auction, I been thinkin' those poor, black people have been stripped of a very basic human right. The right of dignity! What do ya think, Mama? Do ya like the name Dignity for your grandson?"

"Dignity?" Hannah asked wonderingly. "Dignity! Why, yes! It's a fine name!"

"Let me tell her, Willy." Nancy spoke. "Mama,

Willy has picked out a beautiful name, I think. We believe everyone ought to have Dignity. And Willy also wants the baby to be named after the bravest man he ever knew." The room was quiet as she held the sleeping baby out to Hannah. "He's done nursin' now. Would you care to hold your grandson? His full name is Dignity Duffy Stivers."

"Duffy!" Hannah couldn't have been more surprised or pleased. The tears she had been holding back ever since the baby's red face had put in an appearance fell freely now. She held the tiny one out at arm's length and chuckled through her tears. "Dignity Duffy Stivers," she choked, "You're a mighty welcome addition to this family. Mighty welcome indeed."

The baby's parents smiled and sighed contentedly.

Two weeks later Rev. and Mrs. Swank came to the house for dinner after the baby's christening.

"He was just as good as gold, Nancy dear," the parson's wife said. "He never made a whimper."

"I don't think he ever knew he left the house. Willy drove so carefully. He avoided every hole and bump in River Road. 'Twas a lovely day for a ride into Gallipolis," Nancy replied. "And the church looks lovely with the new coat of paint."

"Tom and I were talking about your family's names today, Mrs. Stivers. It's certainly an interesting lot. Willy explained to us about Dignity. But where does the 'Duffy' come from?"

The old lady smiled wistfully as she refilled Mrs. Swank's teacup.

"Well, Duffy was my maiden name. It was also the name we gave our eldest son."

Here Willy interrupted. "I was just a little boy when Duffy went off to war. He died at the battle of Point Pleasant. I'll never forget the night before he left, he pulled me on his lap and said, 'Willy, old man, you take care of Ma and Pa whilst I'm gone. And you remember, little brother, there's some things worth dying for if need be. Freedom, that's one thing.' He was so brave. That's why I wanted to name my son for him. To my way of thinking, a man's dignity is almost as important as his freedom. Mayhap that's another one of those qualities worth dying for - or, more importantly, worth living for! So there, Mrs. Swank, you have the full story of Master Dignity Duffy Stivers' name."

Nancy blushed as she excused herself to the bedroom. "It seems Dignity is feeling hungry," she apologized.

Chapter Four

Dignity's birth came so close to Thanksgiving time that year that what usually had been a time when the whole Stivers family gathered together was bypassed. Libby and Dilly knew that Nancy would neither feel up to travelling nor to having the whole clan gather at her house again. And so it was the consensus that for this year the family would remain apart for the November holiday.

"But Grandma," a letter from Dilly stated, "Please say that you will come to us for Christmas. I spoke with the Captain of the mail packet boat and he says he shall be making a run up the Kanawha on the nineteenth day of December. He will dock overnight at Gallipolis and depart for the return trip from the town center wharf at 8 A.M. on the twentieth. So Frank, True, Prudy, Long and I shall all be at the dock here at Burning Springs awaiting your arrival that afternoon. I know Nancy probably needs your help with little Diggy, but the twins will be inconsolable if you don't accept this invitation."

Hannah stopped for a moment as she read and looked confused.

"Mama," Willy responded, "I think you should go.

It'd do you good to get away for a while. And, as I recall, we did sort of halfway promise Prudy and Long.

"But how will you and Nancy get along without me? Are you strong enough to do all the cooking and cleaning yet, dear?" she addressed her daughter-in-law.

"I will help her. It's a slow time in the building trade since the snows began so early this year," Willy replied. "And other people, you and Papa for example, you got along when us children were born."

Hannah nodded as it began to dawn on her that the little family probably needed time alone as much as she needed time away.

Nancy, sensing Hannah's hurt, said, "Mama, it will be hard to get along without your help. I don't know who shall give Diggy his daily bath but, of a truth, Willy and I feel selfish. We get to have you with us all the time. It sounds as if Dilly will be hurt if you don't go for Christmas. Is there more to the letter?"

"Why, yes, it does continue on the other side of the paper," Hannah answered and then began reading again.

"Mama and Daddy sent word that they will be able to come to our house for Christmas day and the next. He has found a neighbor boy who can do for the cows for a few days at a time. I don't know what it is all about but Mama says in her letter to me that she has a secret that she cannot wait to spring on you. Whatever can it be?"

"Give our love to Uncle Willy and Aunt Nancy and kiss the baby. Bring warm clothing, enough to spend at least a month with us. Your loving granddaughter, Diligence."

"Hmm. Wonder what's going on?" Willy spoke as soon as Hannah had finished the letter. "On the same mail packet boat that brought Dilly's letter to Mama, I got a brief note from Libby. I wasn't going to mention it but since Dilly has already let the cow out of the barn, so to speak, listen to this."

He reached inside the pocket of his waistcoat and pulled out an envelope. Removing the letter he said, "Most of it is just congratulating us on Dignity's birth and inquiring about your health, Mama, but listen to this ending."

"And oh, brother, you *must* see to it that Mama accepts Dilly's Christmas invitation. I have news to share with her that will be such a surprise. I know she'll be as excited as I am about it."

"Whatever can it be?" Hannah mused.

But once the decision had been made that Hannah would indeed go down the Kanawha for the holiday, there wasn't much time to ponder about the surprise. She had been busy for months in the evenings making Christmas gifts for her family. Each of the women were going to receive crocheted lace collars. Hannah had painstakingly seen to it that none of them were even vaguely similar, acknowledging in her own way the difference in their personalities, yet her equal love for them all. The men were to receive fine linen handkerchiefs, lovingly hemmed and with their initial embroidered on the corner. She had decided the twins were too young to appreciate either of these fine gifts and was in a quandary as to what they would like.

"Mama, if the red sky tonight is telling the truth, tomorrow should be a bright, clear day. How about I take you into town to do your shopping? I predict there'll be somethin' at Le Clerque's that'd suit you for the children," Willy suggested.

"Well, I'd rather it be somethin' I could make myself," the old lady mused. "But for the life of me, I can't think of anything and I'm runnin' out of time. All right, I'll go."

The next morning Willy helped his mother down from the spring wagon and escorted her into the store.

"Now, go on with you, son. There's nothing worse than trying to shop with a man a-watchin' every move you make and a-sayin' to every item you pick up, 'That's perfect. Get it.'"

Willy grinned sheepishly, for he knew Hannah was being truthful. "Maybe I'll just take a turn around the town square and see what's new. It's been a time since I've been to town."

After he left, Hannah slowly walked through the store. She looked at clothing, all ready-made. But would a rambunctious ten-year-old like that? At the rear of the store was the tools and hunting section. She almost bypassed it, but then something caught her eye. Ah, yes, here was the perfect gift for Longsuffering. It was a large, very well-made slingshot. The handle was a solid oak Y-shaped affair with a leather pouch to hold the stone. Hannah stood staring at it as if transfixed, with a half-smile on her face.

Mr. Le Clerque repeated his question after clearing his throat loudly. "Meestress Stivers, I said ees dere something I can 'elp you weeth?"

"Oh, yes," Hannah replied trying not to smile too broadly at his accent. "May I see the slingshot?"

"Eet ees for you son, Madame?"

"No, actually I'm thinking of my ten-year-old great-grandson. The reason I didn't hear you is that I was lost in thought. I was remembering a long time ago in Germany when my husband, Will, used a slingshot much like this one to kill food for us. He was an expert with it. I was just wondering . . ." she mused with the beginning of a smile still on her face.

"Eet ees happy I am to see you can theenk of you husband and smile now, Madame. The good book ees correct when it says, *Weeping endureth for a night, but joy comes in the morning,* yes?"

"Yes. I hadn't thought on that particular verse before, Mr. Le Clerque, but indeed it is true." Hannah returned to the business at hand. "How much is the slingshot?"

They settled on a price and the store owner took the slingshot to be wrapped.

Now Hannah turned into the aisle that had toys. She picked up a ball made of various colors of cloth and studied it carefully. She had lots of scraps of material at home and she could find something to stuff it with. Why, a ball such as this would make a nice gift for baby Diggy. Of a truth, 'twould be a long time before he could play with it, but what can a two-month-old baby enjoy? Replacing the ball on the shelf, she vowed to make one in the week remaining before her departure.

With that settled, her thoughts turned to Prudy. There were jackstones in fancy little containers and lengths of rope with brightly painted wooden handles for jumping. But neither of those seemed right. There were corn husk dolls and dried apple dolls and even some cut rag dolls. Hannah was about to despair when she turned into the next aisle of the store.

Here was the fabric and notions department. What caught her eye was the fashion doll. She was made of the finest porcelain. She stood beside the display of new dressmaker's patterns. She was meant to entice the ladies of the town to buy the pattern of the clothing which she modeled in miniature. And what an outfit it was! She was dressed as if for the coldest day in an ankle-length cape of bright blue wool. The hood and armholes were trimmed in ermine fur to match the muff she carried. She also wore tiny shoes buttoned up to her ankles. When Hannah opened the cape to see what was underneath, she gasped. It was a ball gown of red velvet. Mrs. Le Clerque came running over to help.

"Oui, Madame. I weel show you ze dress," she said removing the cape. "You see, eet ees of ze latest fashion weeth ze high neckline treemed een lace. Eet has ze long sleeves coming from ze gathered caplet. And see how ze waistline makes ze letter V een ze front. Now look at ze back," and turning the doll around she continued. "See, there are thirteen of ze tiny pearl buttons coming down her back and she has ze little bustle on her derriere. We not seeing too much of ze bustle in dees land, but my supplier of de patterns, he says eet ees coming. Dey are all de rage in Paris now and some of the fancy ladies een New York City are wearing zem. What you theenk, Madame Stivers? Can I sell to you dees pattern?"

"Oh, no, you don't understand," Hannah replied, coloring slightly. "Yes, it is a lovely pattern, but what I was wondering was if you could sell me the doll?"

"Ze doll? Oh, no, Mam'selle. Ze doll ees not for sale," the portly Mrs. Le Clerque answered with a firm shake of her head that made her curly black hair bounce.

As Hannah began to turn away dejectedly, the store owner rushed over saying to his wife, "What ees dees, mon cherie? Can we not satisfy Mrs. Stivers?"

"She wanted to buy ze doll, not ze pattern. I told her she is not for sale."

"Oh, cherie, you are wrong. Anything een dees store ees for sale, for de right price." His smile told Hannah that even though this man could quote the Bible, he was a businessman to be reckoned with and to watch for in the future. He and his wife argued for a few minutes in French. Then he turned his attention to Hannah.

When he named his price, Hannah began to mentally figure. It was extremely dear, but oh, to see the look on Prudy's face when she opened it! After several minutes a bargain was struck whereby Hannah could have the fashion doll for a certain price plus a quantity of her crocheted collars to be delivered on March first. Hannah was pleased with her bargaining powers until, as she was walking toward the door carrying her purchases, she overheard the owner say, "Mon cherie, do not feel badly. Not one lady een dees frontier town has even looked at ze fashionable patterns or ze doll. We shall make much more money from Mrs. Stivers' fine crocheted collars."

Chuckling to herself, Hannah mumbled, "Mayhap I'm not such a good haggler of prices. But I'm happy with my purchases anyway."

Just then Willy appeared as if out of nowhere. He

seemed agitated as he boosted Hannah into the wagon and inquired about her purchases.

After describing the doll which was all packaged to prevent breakage, and the slingshot, Hannah asked, "What of your walk through town? Is anything new?"

"Yes, there's to be a meeting at Our House, the tavern across the way, tomorrow night. An abolitionist from Philadelphia is going to be here to speak. I want to come."

"Abolitionist? I don't know this term."

"It's a group that wants to abolish slavery. Mama, it's becoming a passion with me I fear. There are horror stories from some of the plantations. It must be stopped." Fervor mounted in his voice.

Hannah smiled at him proudly. "You are so much like your father, William Justice. Follow your heart, son. Do whatever you have to do, no matter what the cost."

"There's some beginning to think the cost will be too tremendous. Some think the issue of slavery will divide America, North from South."

"I hope it doesn't come to that," Hannah replied soberly. "Your father loved America so much."

"But he loved freedom more!" Willy said almost reverently. And then to break the mood he added, "Freedom and Liberty and Justice and Diligence and Truth . . ." Before he completed the list, both mother and son were laughing.

The next week flew by. Willy went to his meeting but didn't say much about it afterward. He just seemed quieter than usual.

All the final preparations were made for Hannah's

departure in the morning. The Ohio branch of the Stivers family celebrated Christmas a few days in advance of the twenty-fifth. Nancy and Willy feigned surprise and expressed their gratitude to Hannah for the handmade gifts. Baby Dignity cooed and smiled at the bright, many-colored, soft ball Hannah held out to him. But Hannah's surprise was very real when Willy gave her a package to open. Inside was a rich brown wool cape. It had a full hood and was completely lined with rabbit fur.

"Oh my," she exclaimed, "I've ne'er seen anything so fine in my life." She turned about like a young girl for them to see the perfect fit. "It is so warm and soft! Where e'er did you get it?"

Nancy smiled shyly. "I made it, Mama Hannah. Willy traded wood for the bunny furs and I stitched them all together. Le Clerque's had the brown wool."

"But when?" gasped the awestruck Hannah. To think that her daughter-in-law should endeavor such a labor of love!

"I worked by lamplight in our room after Diggy's 2 A.M. feeding each night."

Willy didn't want the ladies to end up in tears tonight so he interjected his own brand of humor. "Yes, Mama, I've sacrificed wood and the labor of chopping it and many hours of darkness to sleep by for the cape, so you'd better wear it in good health for many years!"

The next day was so cold and blustery that the Ohio River had white-capped waves rolling eastward as Hannah boarded the mail packet boat in Gallipolis. Nancy and Dignity had not ridden along to see her off due to the weather. She was extremely grateful for the warm cape as she stood on the deck waving to Willy. As he turned the horses toward home, Hannah bowed her head for a moment.

"Lord, bless Willy and Nancy with a wonderful Christmas together. Thank you for their loving care of me. Guide Willy about this anti-slavery movement. Bless little Diggy with good health. Amen."

As she found a seat in the driver's shanty out of the wind, Hannah's thoughts turned down the Kanawha with the packet boat.

"I wonder what Libby's surprise will be," she mused.

Chapter Five

"Christmas never lasts long enough," Longsuffering sighed as he and Prudence worked their way through the mound of dishes. Dilly had outdone herself with preparations for the family Christmas dinner this year. There had been a beautiful, succulent stuffed goose and a baked ham for the main entree. And then there were the mounds of fluffy white mashed potatoes to be drenched in a choice of gravies. Some had chosen to bypass the white potatoes in favor of Libby's famous candied yams. A variety of garden vegetables that had been carefully preserved through the winter months had adorned the table. And Dilly's mother-in-law had brought the traditional dessert of plum pudding.

All the ladies worked together at the 'ridding up' process when the meal had been consumed. But now the grown-ups had retired to the parlor while the twins did the dishes.

"'Tisn't over yet, Long," Prudy responded as she swished the dishrag around in a pan. "We still have the whole afternoon and evening."

"Always seems like a holiday is over once we have to commence workin' again," complained her brother as he carefully placed the best dishes on the table.

"Shame on you, Long," interjected True who had been assigned the task of putting the fine dishes away high in their mother's china cabinet. "How can you complain after all the lovely gifts we received today?"

"Which one of yours do you like best?" Prudy asked Long.

"You do this every year!" the boy grumbled, but a grin had replaced the scowl. "Why do you always want to know what each person's favorite gift is?"

Prudence giggled. "It's just a fun way to remember each one. And somehow it seems to make all the excitement of opening our gifts last longer to remember how we felt as we were surprised. So come on, tell us. Which is your favorite?"

Her twin thought long and hard before he responded. "Oh, Prudy, I really don't know how to answer that question. Each thing is so special in its own way. I like the reed flute that Uncle Willy sent 'cause if you and me practice up on our flutes, we could get real good and play duets."

Without even thinking, True interrupted their conversation to correct her brother's grammar. "You and I, Long. You and I."

Confused, the boy said, "But True, he didn't send you no flute. Just me and Prudy. Wonder how he made 'em anyway?"

The sisters laughed together but Long didn't even realize his blunder as he continued.

"And the slingshot from Great-Grandma will not only be fun, but useful in helping Pa bring in some meat until ever he thinks I'm old 'nuff for my own gun!"

The girls exchanged knowing glances. It was no

secret to them that Long had hoped for a gift of a rifle this year. He'd hidden his disappointment from the adults well, but his siblings knew and understood his feelings.

"I guess I needed the shirts Ma made," he grinned with a shrug. "And I like the ball and stick you girls gave me just fine. But my favorite thing has to be my boots!"

Prudy nodded. "That's what I thought you'd say. And they are fine indeed. Pa said he traded with a riverboat pilot for them when he made that trip clear off to the frontier in the fall. I don't know how they got all the fancy work on them."

"After the leather got carved, they must have used somethin' to dye the horse's head. They sure look like the kind a real cowhand would wear on a cattle drive, huh? I can't wait to show John," he concluded with a reference to their next-door neighbor.

"Well, we needn't even ask you what your favorite thing is, True. If you don't start bending your left hand some, you're bound to drop a dish," Prudy teased the older sister.

"Isn't it beautiful?" True whispered in awe for the hundredth time that day. She held her hand under the lamp so that the ruby ring seemed to catch on fire with light. "I still can't believe it!" she breathed.

The twins rolled their eyes at each other in disgust. "Aw, c'mon. You knew old Bobby Bill was goin' to propose marriage. You two been in love for so long I was beginnin' to wonder if he was ever gonna ask ya." taunted Long.

True bristled. "He just wanted to get his business

established first. And he wanted to get me this.'' Again the left hand was carefully held by the right as she danced a few steps as if caught up in a dream.

Though no one had asked Prudy the same question she herself had posed, she piped up. ''Well, for me it's a tie between the dress Mama made and the doll from Cowma.''

''The smocking on that dress took Mama over a week to do,'' interjected her sister, coming back to reality.

''It is the most beautiful color of pink I've ever seen. Look, there's only the pots and pans left to wash. Best get some clean water,'' she added as she headed for the doorway with the dishpan of now sudsless, greasy water.

''Let's sing,'' said Long as the older sister filled the dishpan with water from the back of the stove while Prudy shaved in more lye soap. And so the three were so deeply involved in carolling that they didn't even hear the commotion at the front parlor door when Libby's long-awaited and much-talked-about surprise appeared.

The older generations were completely relaxed in front of a lovely fire. The candles on the Christmas tree had long since been extinguished. The gifts were neatly stacked in piles for each individual. Libby's husband, Sam, was slouched in a wing-backed chair, feet up on an ottoman, snoring softly. Dilly's Frank was stirring up the lower logs in the fireplace when a loud rapping came at the door.

''I'll go! I'll go!'' shouted Libby and almost danced on the way. She opened the door a crack, whispered to someone and closed it again.

"Mama, whatever are you . . . " Dilly protested, but Libby's face stopped her short.

She was as animated as a young child as she addressed Hannah. "Mama, close your eyes. My surprise has arrived."

Hannah felt foolish but, not wanting to hurt her daughter, she obediently closed her eyes. Thinking the surprise to be some gift, she held out her hands. She heard scurrying around and whispers as the door was opened again. Then suddenly her hands were enveloped in large, strong ones and she was pulled to her feet as a long-remembered voice said, "Hello, old friend."

"Captain Philip!" she shouted as they embraced. "Why, in all my born days, I never!" There were tears in every eye in the room as the reunion was accomplished. "Lands, it's been such a long time!" exclaimed the matriarch of the Stivers' clan.

The old gentleman had aged well in spite of a definite stoop caused by rheumatism. What hair he had was snow-white and he still wore the resplendent uniform of a Sea Captain.

Just then Prudy and Long bounded into the room.

"Who's this?" asked the undaunted boy boldly.

"Sit down, children," Grandma Libby demanded. "I want you to meet the Captain of the ship that brought our Mama and Papa to America. He was like an uncle to me as I grew up. After Marc Woodcutter died, he married Aunt Lucille. Why, he even lived in the clearing with us in the early days of Kelly's Landing. But then he went back to the sea."

"Yes, Phil. What on earth are you doing here in

West Virginia? Whenever I've thought of you over the years, I've envisioned you in some exotic port," Hannah smiled. Periodically she shook her head, still unable to believe he was here.

Finally when the two excited women paused for breath, the stranger spoke. "Well, this time my retirement from the sea is permanent, Miss Hannah. I've recently purchased a packet boat that plies the lower half of the Kanawha. When I came to Kelly's Landing, I ne'er dreamed I'd still find any of you living there. But I would have known Miss Liberty anywhere. She caught me up on all the family history. Miss Hannah, I'm sorry about Duffy all those years ago. And about Will . . ." He struggled visibly with how to show Hannah the true depth of his feeling.

Sam had roused by this time and rose to shake the Captain's hand. Turning toward Hannah he grinned impishly.

"So, Mother Stivers, what do you think of this conniving, scheming daughter of yours? The Captain would have come up to see you a month ago, but Libby wouldn't have it. She had to see your face when the two of you were reunited. She says the Captain is probably the oldest, dearest friend you have left on the earth."

"And she's right!" affirmed his mother-in-law. "But where are our manners, Lib? Introductions need to be made."

As Libby presented her tribe to Captain Philip, Hannah basked in the joy his presence brought. Dilly and True excused themselves to make tea and the children went up to their playroom. Libby asked Phil if he had news of any other long-lost friends from Norfolk. But as he began to fill them in, Hannah put her hand on his arm.

"Wait, Phil. I must know. Why did you give up the sea? You were so unhappy and restless when you tried it before. Will it be better this time?"

"Don't worry, Hannah. I had no real reason to stop sailing before. But this time there's a reason. I've a mission to accomplish. Aye, I can truly say that ne'er in my life have I felt as fulfilled as I have for the last two months as I've run the packet up and down the Kanawha." There was a gleam in his eyes and a set to his jaw that Hannah could not remember seeing before. It bothered her somehow. What did Philip mean? A mission?

But now the Captain turned to Libby. "Do you remember Karla and Chad? And Louisa and Daniel? I saw them just before I began this new venture."

Chapter Six

The same Christmas day had been celebrated very differently some eight hundred miles to the south of the Ohio River. Amber slept soundly on her pallet on the floor by Young Missy's bed. Her mother, Lorena, shook her gently, putting her finger over the sleepy girl's mouth. Beckoning with her finger for Amber to follow, she backed out of the room into the wide hallway.

"What is it, Mama? It's still dark. Young Missy won't be rousing for ever so long." Rubbing her eyes, she glowered at her mother. "I was havin' the bestest dream. I was . . ."

"Hush, chile! It's Christmas mornin'. Surely you 'members what that means. We got tons of work to do and Cook said, 'Fetch every able-bodied house woman we gots.' I didn't want to wake you, baby, but she got specific. 'Lorena, go get that shiftless chile a-you'rn, that Amber. I even kin put her to work this day.'"

The sleepy little girl ran her fingers through her wavy hair. "But what about Young Missy, Mama? Iffen she wakes up an' I ain't here, I's gonna cotch it for sure!"

"Can't be helped, Amber. You's needed in the

kitchen. Now go back in dere and put on your dress. Mind be quiet. Don't go wakin' up Young Missy. Make haste, chile.'' Patting her daughter gently on the rump, Lorena fled on soundless feet to the end of the great hall and down the back stairs through the breezeway to the plantation kitchen.

Amber padded softly back into the room which she shared with Young Missy. She slipped the flour sack dress over her head and efficiently rolled up her pallet, tied it securely and slid it under the edge of the huge four-poster bed where her young mistress snored softly. The first early glow of daylight afforded her a glimpse in Missy's mirror. Her unruly light brown hair looked like the scarecrow's wild mophead down in the river cotton fields. Quickly grabbing her red bandanna from the box under the bed containing her few possessions, she wrapped it tightly around her unruly curls. Deftly sticking a couple hairpins in just the right places, she secured it to her head.

Amber gave one glance at her young mistress to be sure she still slept soundly. As she quietly tiptoed to the door, for a moment her eyes rested longingly on the white kid high-button shoes she had polished last evening and set by Missy's dressing-table chair. Shaking her head as she ran down the hall barefooted she whispered, "Fiddle-de-de. 'Twould take a time and a time to put them on of a mornin'. I'm better off just like I am." Looking every direction including up to the third floor ballroom, and seeing no one, she grinned as she flung her leg over the banister and slid down the last twelve steps on the freshly waxed wood. Even longing for the finer things of life which she would never have couldn't keep Amber's spirits down for long. And so she entered the already crowded kitchen whistling and caught all of them off guard with her perky, "Merry Christmas, Folkses!"

The head cook shook her head and pointed her finger at Amber's nose in perfect syncopated rhythm as she exploded, "Ain't nothin' merry about Christmas 'round here. Jes' means more white folkses 'specting food and usins has to do all de work. Now you go over there by you Mama. 'Rena, get Amber some grits fo' her breakfas'. Then put her to work helpin' you peel the 'taters."

Lorena gave Amber the briefest of hugs and whispered, "Merry Christmas to you, Amber," as she pushed the girl into the chair to her right. Aloud she said, "Eat quick, chile. We's got so much to do!"

As she swallowed the tasteless grits without the luxury of taking time to chew, Amber's blue eyes took in the whole scene before her. Cook and one of the kitchen helpers were ramming stuffing into the necks of a turkey and a goose respectively. Sally, the huge head house maid, was standing over the stove where she was browning a large chunk of roast beef in a dutch oven. Amber could smell ham. When she glanced over at the wall-size fireplace, she noticed Ellen, Big Missy's personal servant, turning the succulent pig on a spit over the fire. Three women from the quarters were rolling pie dough. They had scattered the flour so widely, that from a distance they might have passed for white. Through the window Amber saw that Cook had even put the house men to work. Peter seemed to be humming to himself as he kept the churn handle going up and down to a steady beat. And even Amber's brother, Satin, was busy shelling peas into a bowl so big 'twould take a time and a time to fill it.

The cook's voice brought her up short. "You there, Amber - just 'cause you's a house nigger what belongs to Little Missy now - don' think you ain' gon' do you share of de work. Start peelin' them 'taters, chile. See how many kin you git done afore she calls."

So Amber took the knife her Mama handed her and set to work on the endless stack of potatoes.

"What's Christmas mean, Mama?" she asked.

"Amber, honey, you know what it means. That's the day Jesus Christ was borned into this world. God the Father sent him down from heaven to take away all our sins."

"Must not mean that to the white folks, Mama. They all 'cited bout gifs they gwine get. Young Missy had a whole list of stuff she wants and iffen she don't get it, there'll be the devil to pay."

"Watch how you talk, Amber!" the slave mother admonished. "De devil ain't no laughin' matter. 'Twas him that invented slavery. But anyways, 'bout Christmas - the white folkses believe it's Jesus' birfday same as usins. But they give each other gifts in his memory."

Mother and daughter worked silently for quite a while. The mound of potatoes was half gone when Lorena observed, "The sun is nigh up, chile. I 'spect Young Missy'll be ringin' for you right soon. You done a heap of work already. But try to be extra nice to all de white folks today in honor of Jesus' birfday. Make yo' Mama proud."

"Yes, ma'am." The mulatto child ducked her head

as she always did when any praise came her way. It was rather strange actually. If crossed in any way, Amber would stare eyeball to eyeball with her adversary. But praise befuddled her completely, perhaps because she received so little of it.

Amber had been raised in the quarters down the lane from the big house. Her home was a tiny one-room shack which she shared with her mother and Satin, her brother, who was three years her elder. The walls and roof were barely adequate for shelter but the little house did not lack in cleanliness or love.

Satin had been so named because his skin was just like black satin. Even the palms of his hands were coal black like his hair and eyes. Amber teased him that he could hide in plain view on a dark night as long as he kept his mouth and eyes closed.

Satin was "the spittin' image" of his Daddy, or at least all the field hands said so. Sometimes when Lorena looked at him, she thought her heart would burst with anguish over his lost Daddy. She and Jake had shared that once-in-a-lifetime kind of love when they'd jumped the broom back in 1806. They had privately asked old Brother Josiah to marry them proper in the eyes of God which he had graciously done. But the merriment had all taken place at the broom jump, the only wedding ceremony needed by a slave in the eyes of his white master. Lorena had not wanted to live anymore when Master sold her man down river. Truly had it not been for two-year-old Satin's need of his mama, she might have given up. But that was all ancient history now. For a short time after Jake's sale, Master had taken Lorena into the big house to live and work for

him. But before a year was up, he'd sent her back to the
quarters and she'd become a kitchen helper.

Amber was born in the quarters. Like her brother,
she was named for the color of her skin. She was a pale,
golden color with light brown, wavy hair and eyes as
blue as indigo. Last year when Young Missy had turned
ten, she was given her choice of all the slave girls to
take to the big house and train as her personal maid.
When Amber was chosen from the thirty-some small
girls available, she was excited.

"Mama! She wants me!" she'd squealed.

Lorena had smiled and tried to fake excitement for
her daughter. But, on the inside, another little chunk
broke from her heart and she prayed for discretion on
the part of the folks in the big house.

There was the high tinkling of a bell and Cook
shouted, "She's up. Get going, Amber! Won't do to
keep her waiting, 'specially not on Christmas
mornin'."

Amber laid down the knife and flew to the house
shouting back over her shoulder, "Have a grand day,
everyone!"

Even the sour old cook had to smile. "That chile of
yours is somethin' special, 'Rena. She's like a little ray
of sunshine jis spreadin' joy wherever she goes. Have
you told her anything yet?"

Lorena shook her head as she plunged another
freshly peeled potato into the vat of cold water. "Not
yet. I jis want her to stay happy and sweet as long as she
can."

Sally interrupted, "I'm tellin' you, Lorena. Ya better say somethin' soon. Little Missy and Amber look

more alike with every day that passes. Why, last week I even heard a visitor sayin' when she thought nobody was around, 'Land, it's not hard to tell who that slave girl's father is!' She'd be better off hearin' it from you than anybody else. Doesn't she ever question you?"

"Only once she asked me why Satin is so black and she's so light. Thank heavens that old ewe had just birthed lambs. One white and one black. I told her people is like sheeps. No control over they's color."

All the women chuckled but came right back to the issue at hand. This time it was Ellen who put in her thoughts.

"Best be tellin' her soon, Lorena."

"I'm so ashamed. How's I ever gonna tell her?" With this, Lorena began to sob quietly. Her tears helped to salt the potatoes.

Cook was exasperated. "It's not like it were your fault! Jes' tell her you had no choice. He owns you. You got to do whatever he says."

"But I could have fought him!" sobbed Lorena.

"And been killed! No, sir, you had no choice. No more than Amber herself will have in a few years. Might as well be preparin' her. Haven't you seen the way Master eyes her already?"

Lorena was horrified. "Even he wouldn't do that!"

Just then another bell rang and Ellen yanked off her apron. "Big Missy's up - gotta go."

All conversation ceased as they laid aside the dinner preparations and began breakfast. Ham was sliced and fried, gravy made, eggs scrambled, orange juice squeezed. And all was on the table when Master's family assembled exactly one quarter hour after Big

Missy's bell rang.

"It's been a mighty long day, Amber, but a grand one. Here, I still want you to brush one hundred times," said Little Missy that night as she handed Amber the hairbrush. Staring at her lovely reflection in the mirror as Amber painstakingly brushed her waist-length curls, Young Missy spoke again.

"Did you ever see anything as beautiful as the tree when Papa finally had Peter open the door to the great hall?"

"No'm," replied the slave.

"And isn't my new dolly just bee-you-tiful?"

"Yes'm," Amber methodically tried to determine if the endless questions needed yes or no answers. She was almost asleep on her feet. She'd never put in a harder day. Young Missy had kept her fetching and carrying all day.

"And wasn't it pretty to hear the slaves from the quarters sing for their gifts? You don't feel badly 'cause you didn't get your orange this year, do you? Mama says it's such an honor to get to live in the big house that if we gave you all oranges too, you'd get uppity."

"Yes'm and er . . . No'm." Amber's hands shook as she tried desperately to untangle a curl.

"Ouch! You did that on purpose! I've a mind to tell Mama. You *are* mad about the orange!" The outraged little aristocrat raised her voice.

"I's sorry, Young Missy. And no, ma'am, it weren't on purpose. I's not upset about not gettin' a orange. I's jest bone tired tonight."

"Well, all right. You can unroll your pallet now, but

mind you put away all my new toys and hang my clothes neatly in the press and empty my chamber pot and get fresh water for my morning toilette before you go to sleep. I'll crawl in now. You cover me up. Yes, that's fine. G'night, Amber. Merry Christmas.''

Half an hour later Amber could barely stay awake long enough to pull off her dress and slide into her nightgown before she fell onto her pallet. Immediately she fell into the deep untroubled sleep of a truly tired child.

Thinking she was still awake, Young Missy leaned up on her elbow and whispered, ''Are you awake?'' Mistaking a soft moan for a reply she ventured, ''Amber, do you ever think we look alike? My cousin who came today from Baton Rouge said we are as alike as two peas in a pod. Mama said she had never heard anything so ridiculous. What do you think, Amber?''

The slave girl slept on.

Chapter Seven

The Stivers' conversation lasted late that Christmas night. The Captain caught them up on the lives of the friends whom they had not seen since leaving Virginia forty-some years before. The biggest shock of the evening however, was one for Libby, not Hannah.

"Ah, Libby," the Captain had begun with a gleam in his eye, "Do ye remember yer first love?"

Even after all these years, Libby's face began to glow a bright pink. She reached over and took hold of Sam's hand before she stammered her reply.

"Why, Captain Phil, I'm not sure I know what you mean. Sam is the only man I've ever . . ."

Sensing her daughter's discomfort, Hannah intervened. "Philip, you are incorrigible still. Can't you see you're embarrassing Lib?"

Dilly and Frank and Truth, who had just returned from a long walk with her fiancee, sat up straighter. "Grandma, you're blushing," Truth exclaimed.

"Whatever is this all about?" Dilly inquired.

The Captain was chuckling. "I'm sorry, Lib. But I never dreamed that your family had nary been told of the great unrequited love of your life."

"Philip, stop it! She was just a child," Hannah

reprimanded gently. Libby's frustration was completely disproportionate to the gentle teasing. But truly, Hannah feared her daughter might burst into tears.

Truth was on her knees in front of the Captain now. "Tell . . . Oh, do tell! Who did Grandma love?"

"Only if it's all right with her," said a slightly repentant but still smirking Philip.

There was silence in the room as all eyes turned toward Libby. Finally her irritation seemed to melt behind a translucent smile. Her eyes grew misty as she responded, "Oh, go ahead. All of Virginia knew. I made a complete fool of myself over him! What e'er has become of Little Marc anyhow?"

That night in the privacy of their borrowed room, Sam teased Libby. "So I wasn't the first man in your life after all?"

She threw her pillow at him. "Sam Kelly, that's not true! You were the first and only man for me. Little Marc was just a boy and I was just a little girl at the time. He was Duffy's friend actually. And I can't believe that we never spoke of him. It all seems so long ago to me."

"But you thought you loved him?" Sam was thankful for the darkness which hid his ear-to-ear grin as he continued to tease his wife.

"Yes, I suppose I did think I loved him, until I met you. And, well, yes, I did love him. In much the same way that I loved the whole Woodcutter family. It seems our lives have always been intertwined with that family."

She reached over in the darkness and began to twist her fingers in Sam's graying red hair. "It's sad, isn't it?

To think of Little Marc as a widower? I'm glad for him that he has done so well. Just think, a Federal Judge! But here all these years I've envisioned him with Emily when in truth she died in childbirth just after we left Virginia. Sam, my life has been so full and blessed. It makes me sad to think that Little Marc spent many years alone."

"He should've grabbed you while he had the chance," Sam chuckled, dodging Libby's playful slap in the dark as only one who'd done so for years could have. "But seriously, the Captain said he seems happy now that he's remarried."

"It's just hard for me to imagine Little Marc with a Quaker lady. Saying thee and thou and not believing in fighting."

"Just because he married one doesn't mean he is one, Libby. And, besides, don't be too critical. The Quakers I've known are a fine lot of people. Industrious, kind, peaceful . . . they love the same Lord we do, just in a different way."

"Mmmm . . ." Libby muttered and Sam could tell she was drifting off to sleep.

"Sam," she asked drowsily, "Mama was really surprised, wasn't she?"

"Yes, Miss Liberty, you got her real good."

The next morning the house was all astir as Hannah entered the dining room for breakfast.

Long whined, "But I wanted to see his boat."

"It seems rude to me," True said vehemently as she placed a large plate of steaming home-cured ham in front of her elders. "He should have given us some indication."

"What's wrong?" inquired Hannah.

"It's Captain Philip," Libby cried. "He's gone. Left in the night. No note, no sign of any kind. It's not like him."

Hannah's eyes were wide. "You're right, daughter. It's definitely not like him. But Phil has changed. There's some kind of fervor there that I've ne'er seen in him afore."

Dilly, who up until now had been quietly eating, said, "I should have gotten up. I thought maybe I was dreaming. It was way into the night. I heard three distinct knocks. I thought I heard muffled voices but then it grew still again so quickly, I just turned over and went back to sleep."

"I hope no harm has fallen to Philip," Hannah mused as she pushed her food around on her plate.

Frank seemed aggravated by the whole course of the conversation. "Be reasonable. I'm sure no harm has come to him. He probably just forgot to tell us he would leave early this morning. And Dilly, dear, I'm sure you didn't hear any mysterious knocking in the night. You were undoubtedly dreaming. Now, let's get on with our own plans of the day."

And so the talk ended, but the wondering went on throughout the rest of the visit. Libby and Sam left at noon that day with a promise to keep in touch with them all about Captain Phil. That afternoon Hannah played with Prudy and the doll she'd given her.

"Cowma, Mama wasn't dreaming last night," the little girl said offhandedly as they tried valiantly to hook the tiny high-button shoes on her doll.

"What did you say, Prudy?"

"Mama wasn't dreaming. I heard the three knocks on the door too. But Papa answered the door real quick before I could get to it. I don't think he saw me standing behind the stove. He ran to the door and said, 'Who's there?' And someone outside said, 'A friend with friends.' Papa stepped outside then and I couldn't hear nothing. But soon he went to the guest room and shortly after that Captain Phil left."

Hannah could hardly believe her ears. What on earth had this child seen and heard in the night? Whatever was Phil involved in and how did it all relate to Dilly's husband, Frank? Why were they trying to cover it up with lies?

"Cowma, do you believe me? Cowma . . ."

Prudy's insistent tugging on her sleeve brought Hannah back to reality. She was suddenly very tired and there was the beginning nag of a headache forming behind her eyes. She looked into the earnest blue eyes of Prudy.

"Sweetheart, I think you must have been dreaming. I can't imagine that your Papa would be parading around in the night. Mayhap you just overate yesterday and had you a big nightmare."

"No!" the child stamped her foot in exasperation. "I heard it and I saw it. They said, 'A friend with friends.' Why won't anyone believe me? I tried to talk to Papa but he said I was dreaming too."

Hannah put her hand over her eyes. "Prudy, Cowma has a headache. I need to lie down. Can you go to your Mama and get me some camphor to sniff? Here, take my handkerchief."

So the mystery was forgotten by the ten-year-old as

she scurried to meet the more pressing need. When Dilly appeared at Hannah's door in a rush of concern, the old lady explained that she'd decided to take the next packet boat up the Kanawha. Hannah was grateful that Dilly didn't beg her to stay longer.

"Grandma, believe me, I understand. I know the twins are loud and Long is especially, well - lively? Ornery is a better word," she grinned with a bit of shame on her face. "And I know you well enough to know that you're simply dying to get back to little Dignity."

"Mostly it's my own home I miss," Hannah said as she laid the handkerchief dipped in spirits of camphor across her closed eyelids. "I do hope that as soon as the weather breaks, they'll let me go back to my own place."

Dilly left her when Hannah grew quiet and she hoped she'd waylaid any more questions. For Hannah was absolutely certain that little Prudy had indeed heard and seen something strange. What did it all mean - a friend with friends? Mayhap when she got home she could talk it over with Willy.

The next morning dawned bright and clear. Hannah and the girls were just finishing the breakfast dishes and Dilly was beginning to knead bread dough when they heard Long shouting.

Within a few seconds, Long and his friend, John, burst through the door. "He's back! He's back!" they exclaimed, and everyone knew they meant the Captain.

Frank jumped up from the fire he was building in the oven. "You can finish up here, Dilly. I'll just run down to the wharf to meet the Captain." Grabbing his heavy coat, he was out the door before any of the women could protest.

"What on earth is he so all-fired-up about?" Dilly addressed no one in particular and everyone in general. She and Hannah exchanged confused glances.

The next morning instead of being on the regular mail packet boat, Hannah waved goodbye to her family from the deck of Captain Philip Woodcutter's small steamship, the North Star. Even though it seemed that his original plan had been to go farther south, after a quick conference with Frank, Captain Phil said he could afford to make a special trip up the Ohio to see William Justice Stivers.

Hannah swiped at a tear that dangled on her nose. Prudy always took the leavings so hard. She'd been inconsolable as Hannah tried to explain to her that baby Diggy probably needed her. Even now, she sobbed in her mother's embrace, refusing to look as the ship chugged away from the bank and threaded its way carefully through the large ice chunks.

"But Uncle Willy and Aunt Nancy and baby Diggy get you all the time! And you promised you would stay longer this time. It's not fair." she had cried.

Patting her back, Hannah prayed for some new way to console this special child who reminded Hannah so much of Libby at the same age. There was no kind way to explain to a ten-year-old that an old lady can feel very much 'in the way' in the home of her granddaughter. No way to say, "Prudy, I just want to go home. Home to where I lived with my Will. Home . . ."

But it seemed as if the Almighty had heard her unspoken prayer for an idea began to form. "I know,

Prudy. Whyn't we plan for you to come and stay with me in my own little house this summer? It'd be just the two of us. You'd have me all to yourself.''

It had helped to get them over the crisis. And, Hannah smiled to herself, it would make Willy and Nancy more willing to let her go back home. But now, as she looked back at her family turning away from the dock, a few more tears fell. She wondered if she would ever truly feel at home again anywhere - on any occasion - without Will.

Captain Phil had been busy steering and shouting orders to the two negroes working for him. But now that they were away from the shore and an open stretch of water lay ahead, he turned the wheel over to the larger man and came to sit on a hogshead beside Hannah.

"Are you comfortable, Mistress Stivers?'' he grinned.

"Yes, Captain,'' she retorted. "But if you're free for a moment, I've a question for you.''

"Ask away,'' said he.

"Just this: What does 'A friend with friends' mean to you?''

Philip paled noticeably. He wiped his hand over his eyes in a characteristic way that had always signaled nervousness to Hannah. Turning to her, he tried to look confused. "I have no idea what you mean. What are you talking about?''

Seeing that he was not yet ready to confide in her, Hannah backed off. "Oh, 'tis nothing. Prudy was probably dreaming.'' Changing the subject, she said, "I can hardly wait to introduce you to Willy. The little boy that you remember has grown up to be so much like my Will that it is almost scary. I know you'll be immediate friends.''

Chapter Eight

The long gray days of winter were finally passing. Oh, to be sure, the mornings were still very cold. Outdoors one could see his breath until nearly noon. But the snow had given way to gentle spring rains nearly two months ago. Crocuses and daffodils were in full bloom. There was no ice in the Ohio River. Hannah's red and yellow tulip border along the path from her cottage to the river was preparing to open fully any day.

"Watch him, Mama Hannah," whispered Nancy.

Hannah turned her attention from the window overlooking her cottage to little Dignity in the middle of the floor. He had been cooing and gurgling as he rolled around on the large quilt Nancy laid on the floor for him every day. But now the chubby baby was valiantly working to pull his body to a sitting position. He'd grasped hold of one of the low rungs on Willy's fireside chair. He lay on his back and threw his left leg over his right repeatedly. The happy noises of a minute ago were replaced with grunts of real effort and just the hint of a fussy cry. The two ladies stood transfixed, smiles on each face.

Hannah kept her voice low so as not to distract the

baby as she spoke to Nancy. "Forevermore! I've ne'er seen a baby do such things so young. His daddy was a quick baby being the only one of my children who walked afore he was a year old. But Nancy, upon my word, he's a-tryin' to sit up! And he's just barely five months old."

As she completed the thought, little Dignity not only tried, he did indeed sit up. His round little body rocked forward and back a few times, but he maintained his balance and smiled gleefully. Releasing his hold on the chair rung, he clapped and almost giggled.

Now Hannah addressed her youngest grandson as she leaned over to pick him up. Cuddling him to herself she said, "Yes, Mr. Dignity Duffy Stivers, you're getting to be such a big boy. It's gonna be hard to keep you out of trouble e'er long, I'm thinkin'. We'll need to take the knick-knack dishes off the parlor tables and the antimacassars off'n the chair and couch else you'll be tryin' to eat them."

Nancy stood over the ironing board working on the lovely crocheted pieces. She had laundered them and had them starched stiff as a board. She pushed the hot sad iron around each individual pineapple in the pattern. "His daddy won't miss the antimacassars," she grinned. "He always complains that they're stiff to lean back against. But I tell him that iffen we didn't have them in place, there'd be nasty sweat stains made by his head and hands on all the overstuffed furniture. Besides, they're pretty."

"Mayhap I can show you how to make that popcorn stitch on the edging one of these evenings afore I move back home," Hannah replied. "But is there a bottle fixed for this little monkey? Look at him rubbin' his eyes. Nap time, it looks like.''

Nancy released the sad iron from the handle and put it back on the burner of the big black stove to reheat. Before she replaced it with the hot one, she took the baby's bottle out of the pan of water and tested it on her wrist.

"Just right," she announced and reached for the baby.

"Oh, no, let me," protested the mother-in-law. And so Nancy continued to iron the lacy crocheted antimacassars while Hannah rocked the little boy to sleep.

A shadow fell across Nancy's face as she spoke quietly. "I still miss nursing him," she said.

"Now quit your worrying. Lots of women get milk fever. We should just be glad that you recovered as quickly as you did, and that this greedy piglet took to cow's milk as easily as he did. Why, his daddy had to be raised on goat's milk.''

She talked on as Nancy turned back to the ironing board with a smile. Hannah loved to talk about the days back in Norfolk, Virginia, when the children were small and they'd had goats for Willy's sake. Truly, she would miss this grand lady when she moved back down the hill to her own cottage soon. Willy thought it was best to let his mother have her way in this. They could check on her every day. And besides, it would free up Hannah's room just off the kitchen for Willy's venture.

❋ ❋ ❋ ❋ ❋

Looking back, Hannah thought three events stood

out in her mind from that spring and early summer. And they had happened in such quick succession that an old lady hardly had time to catch her breath in between.

The first was the momentous day when she'd been allowed to move back to her own little cottage. The weather seemed to go from a damp, cool spring directly into a hot summer overnight. With the warm, drier air and the promise of living on her own again, Hannah's ever-present stiffness and soreness from rheumatism had nearly vanished. After a few days of airing out and carrying supplies and her personal items back down the hill, Hannah was back home.

"I've stacked the woodbox as full as I dare," Willy said as he hovered near the doorway. "And I've brought ya up a good week's supply of stuff from the cellar." He looked at the trap door entrance to the cellar just inside the front door worriedly. "Mama, now promise me that when you need anything, you'll ring the dinner bell out on the porch. I don't want you trying to lift that door or going down cellar for anything, ya hear?"

"Aach, Willy. Be off with you!" Hannah playfully pushed him out the door. "I may be eighty-six years old but I'm perfectly capable of doing for myself. And I guess I've got sense enough to know what I should or shouldn't do." Her tone softened. "We'll see each other every day, son. I'm grateful, Willy - I truly am - for all you and Nancy have done. I will miss you and I hope you'll bring Diggy down real often. But now go home to your family and let me enjoy my home."

And truly, it did feel like home again. Oh, she knew she would never get over missing Will. She felt his presence so keenly in these rooms though the family had thoughtfully removed all his clothing and personal items that would make it hard for her. Of a truth, she had to force herself not to talk to him, he felt so near. But the pain had gone out of that feeling in the months she'd lived with Willy. Once all she could see was the suffering, dying form of her husband; but now she remembered the vital, robust man who had moved here with her forty-six years before and carved this home out of the wilderness that was to become Ohio.

She'd just grown accustomed to her new life when the mail packet had brought grand, exciting news from down the Kanawha.

"Dear Great-Grandmother, Great-Uncle Willy, Great-Aunt Nancy, and, of course, dearest cousin, Dignity," the letter began with a flourish.

"Trust Truth, the schoolmarm, to get the relationships exactly correct to the very jots and tittles," Willy mumbled and received a glare from his wife. They were all seated in Hannah's front room around the lamp as Nancy read the letter.

"As you will no doubt remember, Robert William Longtree gave me a beautiful ruby ring at Christmas and asked me to be his wife."

Willy, in an ornery mood, interrupted again, "Robert William. La-de-dah! Since when is he anything but Bobby Bill, the boy who's been moonstruck with True for about four years?"

"Willy, please!" Hannah said as she lovingly patted Diggy on the back, awaiting a burp. "Go on, Nancy."

"Let's see . . . asked me to be his wife. The bans have been read for the first time at the church service this morning, so this letter is to let you know that the wedding date has been set for June 3, 1821. I realize that is less than a fortnight away and I trust this will not be an inconvenience for any of you to arrange to be able to come. For I do so dearly hope that all of my wonderful family can be here to celebrate my nuptials with me.''

''Mom says to tell you that . . .''

''Mom?'' Hannah choked in disgust. ''Whenever did she begin to call her mother that? I just hate to hear young people use this new-fangled slang.''

''Oh, Mama,'' Willy replied. ''You know Truth. She's always prided herself on being very up-to-date. I doubt she means any disrespect. I hear all the young people in Gallipolis referring to their parents as Mom and Dad.''

''And to think she gave Prudy a rough time for calling me Cowma!'' The old lady shook her head. ''Well, Nancy, go on. What is it that *Mom* says to tell us?''

''That we have room for all of you to stay. Captain Phil will dock the North Star right at the foot of your sidewalk early on the morning of June second. The wedding will be the next day. And Captain Phil will take you all home after church on Sunday, June fourth. Dad has it all arranged so there will be no cost to any of you.''

Chapter Nine

The second momentous event in Hannah's memory of that summer was the wedding. Coming as it did just ·three weeks after she'd moved home, there had been little time to prepare. Nancy had rushed into town to buy yard goods to make herself a new dress since none of the Mother Hubbards she'd worn the previous summer fitted her slim-again body. Hannah had spent every waking moment from delivery of the letter until the wedding ten days later in crocheting a lovely afghan for her gift to the bride and groom.

The ceremony was beautiful. It was held in the church in Burning Springs on the evening of June third. The sanctuary was aglow in candlelight as Frank escorted True down the aisle in a creation of white satin and lace and seed pearls which would always be remembered as Dilly's finest creation.

Hannah's mind floated back over the years to the white-spired church in Norfolk. Instead of hearing Truth and Bobby Bill repeat their vows, it was her own voice she remembered and it was Will's black eyes she saw as the lovely words from the book of Ruth were repeated.

Whither thou goest, I will go, and where thou lodgest,

I will lodge. Thy people shall be my people and thy God my God.

The notes from the newly installed pipe organ brought Hannah back to reality.

That evening and the next day was such a hubbub of activity that it was a relief to Hannah when Captain Phil docked the boat and insisted on escorting her up to her cabin the next evening. She made them coffee and brought blueberry pie from the safe in the pantry. They chatted amicably as old friends do and then Phil noticed that the sun was a giant orange ball in the west.

"It's time for me to be on my way. I'll stop again soon, Hannah. Just now I want to run up and say goodbye to Willy. He's a wonderful young man, you know."

Hannah waved with a smile as he started up the hill. Willy's house was set in a circle of trees. It must be getting dark in the shade for as she watched, she saw a lighted candle being placed in the front parlor window. Hannah turned back to her own dear cottage, happy that her oldest friend held her son in such high esteem that he stopped here regularly to visit with Willy.

The third event still left Hannah rather shaken. She had ridden into town with Willy to get a few things for her larder. Prudy was to come in a week for the long-promised visit with her Cowma. Hannah needed sugar and vanilla to create Prudy's favorite cookies. And she also hoped there might be some more of the exquisite fashions which would just fit Prudy's doll. Hannah realized guiltily that she probably showed favoritism to this great-grandchild, but how could she help it when Prudy was so very much like her grandmother, Libby, had been at the same age?

Hannah stood in line at Le Clerque's with her arms full of would-be purchases. The door opened and a lovely young woman dressed all in gray with only a wide white collar to relieve the drabness entered. She held her small son's hand and stated in a cool voice, "Put thine other hand in thy pocket, Lemuel. Thy father may be rich but there's no use in us paying for any unwanted items because thy careless hand might break something." The strange speech of the Quaker lady brought stares from the whole store.

Then it was Hannah's turn at the counter. She made her purchases and exited the store. As she was climbing up onto the buckboard with Willy's help, a man emerged from a nearby carriage.

"Wait!" he shouted as he ran toward them. "Can it be?" he stammered. "You look so much like a lady I knew long ago. She wasn't my real aunt but our families were so close. I always called her Aunt Hannah Stivers."

Before the speech was finished, there were tears coursing down her cheeks. "Forevermore! Little Marc! I ne'er thought I'd e'er see you this side of Heaven. What on earth . . ."

Within a few minutes Hannah and Willy had been invited to one of the newest homes in Gallipolis. It sat right next to the town square. It was three stories on the back river side, with just two stories facing the street, so steep was the hill it was built on.

Little Marc's demure Quaker wife, Hope, prepared a lovely tea in short order with the help of their seemingly endless brood of children. Lemuel, the one Hope had warned in the store, was the only one Hannah had any hope of remembering. The older children, three girls and two boys, flitted about more quietly than any young people Hannah had ever seen. Hope was a gentle lady. Within moments after making her acquaintance, one felt that if she had not said *thee and thou* it would seem strange.

Little Marc explained that his Federal Judgeship forced him to make many trips to the state capital at Marietta and sometimes even to the new town on the western edge of Ohio, Cincinnati. "So I wanted to settle somewhere in between. Gallipolis seemed logical. And I ne'er dreamed it would put me close to you." He and Hannah recalled days of yore with such affection that Willy and Hope never felt left out. But the day grew short and it was time to leave.

As Willy urged the horses homeward, he mumbled, "I can't imagine it."

"Can't imagine what, son?"

"That blasted statue!"

Hannah recoiled at the vehemence of his tone. "Why, son, whatever do you mean?"

"I suppose you didn't even see it. It was by the drive which led around back to the barn at your friend, Marc's, house. They had one of those awful statues of a little Negro slave boy all dressed in his finest livery. In his hand he's supposed to hold a lantern but this one had the lantern broken off. Just an empty hand. When we first met them, I thought, 'Ah, Quakers! They will be sympathetic to our abolitionist cause.' But surely, no one who truly believes that all men are created equal would have one of those statues decorate their home."

"Willy, try not to carry on so. After all, as a Federal Judge, I'm sure Little Marc had to swear to uphold that fugitive slave law that I'm always hearing you go on about. So, no, I don't suppose they are abolitionists."

"That law's been on the books since 1793. It needs to be repealed so desperately. But I've just about decided working within the law is not the best way to handle this. Sometimes a man has to go outside the law!" The last was said with a crack of the whip that started the horses galloping.

"Willy!" Now it was Hannah's turn to raise her voice. "Your father would be appalled at you for cruelty to these poor horses. Slow down, son! I've ne'er seen you get so upset. And all over some silly statue. Take it easy, son. I know you feel deeply about this slavery issue, but if Little Marc and Hope don't agree with you, that doesn't make them bad people. Mayhap they just don't feel . . ." But her voice trailed off for the scowl on Willy's face did not lessen.

Hannah had not spoken to Willy any more of the incident, but every day she prayed that her son would not do anything foolish in his zeal against slavery.

She smiled as she remembered again the reminiscing with Little Marc. His wife had returned her call three days ago bringing delicious Gingerbread Men cookies. "I thought your little great-granddaughter would enjoy them," she smiled. "When is it that she is to arrive?"

So much had happened so fast that even Hannah was surprised when she answered, "Tomorrow!"

Chapter Ten

"Oh, Cowma, I thought that old boat would never get here," exclaimed Prudy as she returned Hannah's welcoming hug.

"Well, a watched kettle seems ne'er to boil, little one. Patience is something you and I are both short of, I fear. Was your trip up the Kanawha pleasant?" she asked as they waited for the roustabout to carry Prudy's bag to the spring wagon.

"Pleasant enough, I suspect. But 'twas awfully long, it seemed to me. Once we rounded the curve into the mighty Ohio, it got fearsome interesting though. My, but Gallipolis just seems to grow and grow. And, anyway, the Ohio is ever so much bigger and flows faster than the Kanawha."

Hannah smiled. "Mayhap you just got excited once you got into the Ohio 'cause you knew you were almost here. Too bad you couldn't have come on the North Star. Captain Philip would probably have swung east at the mouth of the river and delivered you directly to my door."

Prudy nodded, serious-faced. "Papa always gets sort of strange when we mention Captain Philip. I asked him when the North Star would be coming north again, thinking I'd a-been willing to wait a couple days in order to ride with the Captain. I mean, I was anxious to get here, Cowma . . . but I bet the Captain would have even let me drive the boat or something.''

Hannah chuckled, remembering her very first encounter with Philip Woodcutter over fifty years before. ''No, Prudy, I doubt that. Of course, he's had to change his ways concerning women aboard his ship. But something tells me that he still wouldn't allow a female person to steer.'' Realizing, as she often did lately, that she was living too much in the past, she asked, ''Where is Captain Phil anyway? We haven't heard from him in a time and a time.''

''I don't know. Papa said likely he wouldn't be coming north for a spell. Said he had a special kind of work detaining him south of where we live. Even south of where Grandma Libby lives down at Kelly's Creek. Papa always acts real mysterious and wants to change the subject quickly whenever we mention the Captain. Wonder why?''

Hannah rubbed her forehead with her hand, feeling the grooves deep thinking caused as she contemplated Prudy's words. This child was so insightful and quick. Hannah realized it would take all her intellect to stay even one step ahead of her great-granddaughter for this month-long visit they were to enjoy.

''There, your bags are loaded in the wagon. Willy had some purchases to make at Le Clerque's Mercantile over at the square. We are all to take afternoon tea yonder at the big new home of Judge Marc and Hope Woodcutter. Let's be off then,'' she said taking Prudy's hand.

Prudy skipped every third or fourth step and bounced with enthusiasm. "Do they have children? Surely they must 'cause it's a mighty big house. Oh, I hope I shan't spill anything at tea and embarrass you. Do they have girls? Sometimes I get so tired of just having Longsuffering to play with. I mean, he's a good brother, but . . ."

"Shh. We're almost there. I need to explain to you. These are lovely people. And, yes, they have three daughters and three sons. But Prudy, these people are Quakers so that means they dress plainer and talk differently than we do. So try not to act too surprised."

This last was said as they mounted the steps to Judge Marc's home. Before they'd even knocked, the door swung wide. Hope stood before them beaming.

"Come in, come in, new friends." She reached forward and surprised Hannah with a kiss on the cheek. "Oh, Aunt Hannah, may I call thee that? Marcus does and it's automatic with me, I fear. But, thee'll never know how thrilled we are to be close to thee and thy family. After we left Williamsburg and moved up to Richmond, Marcus always seemed sort of lost. But now that he has been appointed to this district and we are settled here in Ohio, he's much more content. But listen to me rattle on. Where are my manners?" Looking down at the red-haired girl at Hannah's side she said, "Thee must be Prudence. We are so pleased to make thine acquaintance. Come on in. The girls have the tea all ready."

Prudy's eyes grew rounder as she looked past her hostess to the extremely plain, almost crude-looking interior of this lovely home. Why, the dining room suite was nothing more than a table which looked as if it belonged in a kitchen to make bread or pies on. There were eight extremely plain, straight wooden chairs. There was nothing ornamental or pretty in the room. The plain wrought iron sconces on the walls were obviously functional only. No flowers or candles were on the table or mirrors or portraits on the walls. As Prudy tried to remember that, indeed, a very rich Federal Judge lived here, her peripheral vision caught action. Turning slightly, she saw three girls carrying cakes and assorted goodies to the table. The girls, though varied in size, were dressed in identical black dresses with wide, white collars. All three had their hair pulled back into uncomely, severe, round buns. But they all smiled as their mother made the necessary introductions.

"Girls, this is Mistress Hannah's great-granddaughter, Prudence. Prudence, my three daughters. Constance, who like thee, is almost eleven." This was said with a slight smile and a wink at Hannah above the girls' heads. "Then there's Jerusha who is fourteen. And Naomi who is almost twenty."

As they were introduced, the group of ladies had circled the table and pulled out the chairs to be seated. "The boys are out back fishing, Mama. They said to tell thee that they did not care for any tea today," volunteered Jerusha.

Addressing Hannah, Hope asked, "But what of thy son? Shall we await his arrival?"

"Oh, I think not. When he gets to talking with gentlemen at the stores on the square, I never know when to expect him."

"Then let us thank God for our tea," Hope instructed. All the heads bowed but no one prayed. Prudy opened an eye. All of the Woodcutter ladies' lips moved but no sound came forth. She turned her curious eyes to Hannah who likewise was peeking during prayer. Hannah had a very questioning look on her face and shrugged her shoulders. Putting a finger to her lips, she closed her eyes. So Prudy did the same.

After a time, Prudy felt a nudge against her leg from Hannah. Opening her eyes, she found the Woodcutter ladies were now pouring tea and passing the plates of cakes and cookies.

"I like thy name, Prudence." The shy Constance spoke.

"I like yours too, Constance. But you can call me Prudy. Out in the wagon I've got my best dolly. Maybe we can play with it later."

Constance's eyes seemed lit from within but Hope interjected, "Eat thy food, girls. Then thou canst show our guest the rest of the house, Constance."

As the tea continued, true friendships were beginning. Hannah was telling Hope about the local shop owners and the girls were talking of school when Prudy tried to draw the shyest girl of all into the circle.

"Naomi, being twenty years old, how long have you been a spinster?"

"I beg thy pardon," the girl retorted, face reddening.

"A spinster. How long have you been? My sister, Truth, just married this summer. She's only eighteen but she'd been a spinster already for five years."

Hope, a bit indignant herself, felt she must intercede

for the gentle Naomi. "Prudence, this is a very sore spot with our Naomi. No one likes to be called a spinster any more. Thee should learn to think before thee opens thy mouth."

Immediate tears filled Prudy's eyes. "But Ma'am, I never meant no harm. I'm sorry, Naomi. I just wondered when you finished your last quilt."

Cowma came to her rescue. "I'm afraid Prudy isn't aware that *spinster* has come to be a derogatory word in some circles. 'Tis a stupid custom, anyway, don't you agree, Hope?"

"Yes, why must a girl stop at twelve quilts in her chest and do nothing but spin the wool in the home until some boy asks for her hand in marriage? Why, there's been plenty of times I could have used more than my original twelve quilts with this big family."

Here Jerusha entered the conversation. "And if we are only allowed to make twelve quilts before marriage, then why is it so important that we begin to quilt so young? I finished my twelfth quilt nigh a year ago. I'm only fourteen and I've been a spinster for almost a year."

Constance interrupted, "I bet a democrat made up the rule."

Hope exploded. "That will do, Constance! Thou dost not bet and thy father is a democrat. Thou and Miss Prudence may be excused to explore the house."

The two little girls left the room with heads down. But soon, laughter drifted up the stairs to the ladies drinking tea.

"Constance hath need of a suitable playmate her age. Perhaps your Prudence could come and visit her betimes," Hope said.

"Whyn't you let her come home with us now?" ventured Hannah. "I fear Prudy may soon grow tired of just her old great-grandmother to play with."

And so it was that when Willy came to the door to get his mother and Prudy, there was an extra valise to be piled on the buckboard. The two girls had become fast friends and were giggling together in the back as they headed out River Road.

As the wagon passed the carriage road around back of the great house, Prudy nearly shouted in her excitement.

"Oh, look! The darling little slave boy! Isn't he cute?"

Willy looked at the statue in disgust but noticed that something had been added. In the hand from which the lantern had been broken, the little Negro boy held a miniature American flag.

"Oh, yes," Constance agreed with Prudy's assessment of the statue. "We have taken the little boy statue with us wherever we lived. But he doesn't always hold the flag in his hand. Only when Papa is away doing his judge job."

Hannah and Willy looked at each other inquiringly. These Quakers certainly had a lot of queer practices.

"Do you know how long your Papa will be gone?" Prudy asked.

"Well, no. But he always lets us know by cable or a letter or some way when he will return. We put the flag into the statue's hand when he leaves and when Mama gets word that he is returning, we remove the flag a day in advance," Constance said.

"Strange custom," Hannah whispered.

"Hmmm . . . I wonder," mumbled Willy.

Chapter Eleven

It had been arranged by the grown-ups that Constance would spend Friday, Saturday and Sunday with Prudence and Hannah. Willy would take the girls back to the Woodcutter mansion early Monday morning where they would play together all day and then Prudence would return home with Willy at the end of the day.

Never were two girls more perfectly matched. "They're soul sisters," Hannah said to Nancy on Saturday afternoon when they had gone up to show Baby Dignity to Constance.

"It's nice, Mama Hannah. I doubt our Prudy has had many playmates her own age. Oh, of course, she always has Long. But there's something special about a girlfriend. When I was about her age, I had a best friend named Fran. We always said we were kindred spirits."

Hannah watched wistfully out the window as the girls raced for the woods. "Yes, I love to see Prudy have such fun. When I was her age, there was no joy in my life."

Nancy turned the topic to one of more imminent concern. "But what about her being a Quaker? What will you do tomorrow? Will she attend services with all

of us? And aren't Quakers very strict regarding Sunday
- you know, keeping the Sabbath?''

"Her mother said she might attend our church and
Sunday School. As for the activity in the afternoon, I
intend to let those two do anything they want. They've
been extremely well-behaved so far. And Constance is
such a joy to watch as she discovers things she's ne'er
been exposed to. You should have seen her with
Prudy's fashion doll,'' Hannah chuckled. "I tell you, I
really thought those darling blue Woodcutter eyes
would pop clean out of her head. For a while she just
watched as Prudy undressed her and put on her night-
shirt and cap preparing the doll for bed. Then Prudy
generously offered to let Connie do the nightly ritual-
istic brushing of its hair. She only hesitated for a
minute and said with a giggle, 'If it's a sin, I'll have to
be sorry later. But right now give me the brush!'''

Nancy laughed as she poured scalding water into the
teapot to prepare a mid-afternoon treat. "Did you have
trouble getting them to bed last night? I remember
when e'er my friend, Fran, and I slept over we would
talk and giggle until my Pa threatened us with a hickory
stick switching."

As Hannah poured the tea, she explained, "I don't
think they did too bad. They slept in the living room
before the fire. To tell the truth, my failing hearing
might be a blessing, though. From my room I didn't
hear a thing."

The two girls rambled through the nearby woods all
afternoon. After supper dishes were washed and put
away, Prudy asked if they might go down the path and
play by the Ohio River.

"Just don't do anything dare-devilish, and come when I ring the bell," Grandma Hannah replied. Of a truth, she needed some peace and quiet and a break from the constant chatter of the girls.

They had skipped stones, looked for shells along the beach, and though they never would admit it, they were beginning to grow a bit weary.

Sinking down onto the warm sand, Prudy said, "Tell me about your religion, Connie."

"Well, I know thee callest us Quakers, but we prefer to call ourselves *Friends*."

But Prudy never learned any more about Connie's beliefs that evening. For that one sentence had sparked a long-buried memory in Prudy's mind. She rolled over on the sand so that she could look upward at the orange-tinted sky through the long, slender leaves of the willow tree above them. Her face seemed lit from within with a glow that matched the sky. Interrupting Constance she said, "Wait a minute, Con. I just have to ask you something while I've got it in my mind. You said your religion is called *Friends*. Last Christmas there was a real strange thing happened at my house. I'll tell you the whole story - but I just have to know. Have you ever heard anything like 'A friend with friends' used as some sort of secret code?"

Prudy was not prepared for the change that came over her friend. She sat up straight and looked around furtively. "Shhh. Thee mustn't say that aloud. Wherever did thee hear it?"

Prudy sat up too and immediately mimicked her friend. Glancing back up the path, she suddenly felt silly. "There's no one here exceptin' us. No one could possibly hear. So, tell me, Con. What does 'A friend with friends' mean? I heard someone say it late at night through a locked door to my Papa. And then he went and woke up a friend of ours, Captain Phil . . .''

Before she could go on, Connie was on her feet, bouncing around excitedly, but still looking frightened out of her wits. "Oh, dost thou know what this means? Thy father and my mother are both in it. I didn't know thee knew Captain Phil. But Prudy, we've got to be careful, doesn't thee see? 'Cause it's all such a huge secret!''

Prudy grabbed her friend's arm. "What in the name of heaven are you talking about? *What* is such a huge secret?''

But the girls had been so intent on their conversation that they'd missed the first ringing of Hannah's bell. Now it rang on in earnest.

"Oh, dear, we have to go. Cowma will worry. We must run but when we get there you can . . .''

"No!'' the agitated Connie responded. "It's such a special secret that not all grown-ups know. Thy grandmother may not. We'll have to wait until bedtime.''

"Prudence! Constance! Come home, girls! It's gettin' dark.'' Hannah shouted from the cabin porch up the hill.

"Coming, Cowma!'' Prudy responded in the loudest voice she could muster. "Okay, then, bedtime!'' she whispered to Connie as they ran up the path.

Would this evening never end? Usually Prudy would have been thrilled that Hannah allowed her to stay up so long past lamp-lighting time. Trying to be a good hostess and grandmother, Hannah had the popper full of corn and three wonderful apples hanging on a string when the girls puffed in from their romp by the river.

"We'll hang this cord, just so, above the fire," Hannah instructed, being very careful that the girls keep their distance from the blaze. "Prudy, you take the first turn at shaking the corn and when your arm is nigh ready to drop off, let Constance take over," she said as she handed the long-handled popcorn popper to her great-granddaughter. "Would you like to sing as we ready our snacks?"

The two young voices and the one growing rather raspy joined in several songs that were popular. Some had the right beat to lend themselves perfectly to the shaking of the popcorn. They sang some hymns and Constance knew every one as well as they did. Then she said, "Dost thou know this song?"

Her low contralto sounded plaintive as she began falteringly, but as the song continued, it grew full and tremulous.

> *When Israel was in Egypt land - Let my people go,*
>
> *Oppressed so hard they could not stand - Let my people go.*
>
> *Go down, Moses, Way down in Egypt land.*
>
> *Go down, Moses - Let my people go.*

Hannah began to hum along as Connie sang the second verse.

> *Massa sleep in de feather bed, Nigger sleep on de floor,*
>
> *When we gets to Canaan land - There'll be no slave no more.*
>
> *Go down, Moses, Way down in Egypt land.*

Go down, Moses - Let my people go.

Prudy shivered. "Ooh, it's beautiful, but the tune is sort of strange and spooky. I've ne'er heard it before. Let's sing something happy."

"Sounds to me as if the popcorn's ready. Let's eat," the grandmother said.

They went to the kitchen to get bowls for the corn, but Hannah seemed a bit depressed.

"Where e'er did you learn that song, Constance? The only place I ever heard it before was a big darky slave named Samantha used to sing it when I first came to America."

The little girl's face reddened. "I don't rightly know where I learned it, Ma'am. But what about the apples?"

Hannah hurried to retrieve the apples from the top of the fireplace. They were baked to perfection, just a bit of the juice beginning to ooze out.

"Prudy, you run down to the cellar and get us cold milk to drink."

Prudy went to the living room and deftly lifted the trap door near the front door. Carrying a candle to light her way, she bounced down the steps. As always, when she arrived at the foot of the stairs, she marvelled at this room. Her great-grandfather must have been a genius to devise such a room. He'd loved Hannah so much that he didn't want her to venture outside in the winter weather. What appeared to be a typical cellar for vegetable storage was also an underground tunnel to the springhouse which sat several yards up the hill. Having done so many times, Prudy lifted the latch on the end cupboard and, as it swung away to the right, she followed the tunnel to the basement of the springhouse where she retrieved a jug of fresh milk. On her return trip, she pushed the cupboard back and latched it carefully. So often Cowma had reminded her, "It'll keep varmints from running from the springhouse to the cellar and vice-versa." As she came back up the steps into the living room, Cowma was talking.

"And so you see, Miss Constance, your father, Marc, and my oldest son, Duffy, were very best of friends."

"Just like me and Prudy," the exuberant girl exclaimed.

"Tell us a story, Cowma," begged Prudy as she forked a bite of the delicious warm apple.

"Tell me about my Papa when he was little," Constance pleaded.

And so the evening continued around the kitchen table. The apples were gone and the milk jug was empty. Only a few kernels of unpopped corn remained in the bowls. Grandmother Hannah stifled a yawn as she stood and began to stack the dishes near the dry sink.

"You girls best get into your nighties. I'll spread the pallets by the fire while you change."

Prudy was so excited as they prepared for bed that she had to stifle a nervous giggle. She was about to be told some great secret that not even all grown-ups knew. With lantern in hand, the three ladies made their way to the privy out back.

"Hmmm. That candle is in the window of my old room at Willy's again. We ne'er lit one while I lived there," Hannah noticed.

"Ouch!" Prudy said disgustedly for Constance had

jabbed her in the ribs. When she looked at her in the lantern light, she had her finger over her mouth though her eyes were dancing.

"I must have stepped on a stone," Prudy lied to her great-grandmother while staring at her friend with questioning eyes.

Finally settled for the night, the girls waited until they heard Hannah's soft snoring before the revelation began.

Constance leaned up on one arm in front of the fire and looked deeply into Prudy's eyes. "Hast thou ever heard of the Underground Railroad?" she began.

Chapter Twelve

At approximately the same time that Prudy learned about the Underground Railroad, many miles to the south, Amber made an equally shocking discovery. It happened on the day of Young Missy's birthday celebration. The plantation had been all in a hubbub for weeks planning this party. It was a barbecue to which everyone in the area who was important was invited.

Some of the neighboring women were overheard complaining about the party.

"Howsomever are the rest of us ever supposed to keep our daughters happy when they have their birthdays?" said a panting, heavy-set lady with ringlets of damp blonde curls.

"Well, in my opinion, it's nigh onto sinful the way they indulge every whim of this child. The barbecue alone must have cost - why - who knows how much? My Henry said there was an entire cow plus the normal pork over the pit, when he brought me my plate at noon," said a mousey looking little woman in a muslin dress that obviously had been let out on two different occasions. "Keep that palm branch moving, nigger. Lands, did you ever see a hotter day?"

The ladies were in the upper bedrooms of the mansion taking their customary naps during the afternoon. Amber had been assigned by Big Missy to be one of the fanners in the adults' rooms. She would have much preferred to fan Young Missy and her friends but, of course, she obeyed her orders without questioning. Big Missy had been in such a state planning this party that it surely wouldn't have been wise to cross her. And so it was that while she fanned, she couldn't help but overhear their gossip. It was all she could do to keep the stupid, solemn look on her face which was expected by all.

Now Mrs. Quinlan spoke in her nasty nasal twang. "Never has a child been so spoiled in my opinion. That carriage and set of four matched ponies is a gift for a queen, not a little girl in the backwoods of Louisiana. The governor's children probably don't have . . ."

"Shhh. Keep your voice down," one of the other women hissed. "She could come back at any time."

"Niggers! Speed those fans. I'm about to perish, I'm so hot!" said the mousey one.

Amber moved the palm leaf as fast as she could but Lucy, the other slave girl, just kept a steady pace.

"Pardon me, ma'am, but iffen you would loosen your stays, you'd prob'ly be breathin' easier."

Amber sucked in her breath at Lucy's insolence. If the mousey lady chose to tattle, Lucy would be in for a whipping. That was for sure!

The lady glared at Lucy and went on talking to the neighbors who shared her bed. "Listen to that. Even the niggers here are uppity."

The blonde interjected her thoughts. "My husband said he thinks the reason they spoil the girl so is 'cause they've got no others. And after that last little boy died at birth and 'her highness' was so sick, it's my guess there's no hope of ever havin' any more children.''

Another lady spoke from across the room. Amber couldn't see clearly who she was because the shades were down to try to cool the room.

"'Her highness' as you call her is our hostess, and I think some people in this room should remember that. I saw that none of you were too good to eat their barbecue. After all, if you thought the party was too elaborate for the child, well . . . no one made you come. If you ask me, even though they're the richest in the whole county, I think this family is to be pitied.''

"Pitied! Why on earth should we pity people who put on so many airs?'' Mrs. Quinlan asked.

"Because what she said a minute ago is true. There can't ever be any more children in this house. I have it straight from Mrs. Doctor Steiner that he had to operate on her after the baby boy.'' The lady who volunteered this information seemed to genuinely like her hostess but, as with nearly all the gentle ladies of the south, she also relished knowing a juicy morsel of gossip that the others did not know. "Straight from Mrs. Doctor Steiner,'' she repeated.

All grew quiet except for the palmetto branches for such a spell that Amber thought they had all fallen asleep. Her own eyes were heavy. Her arms ached.

Then the chubby blonde leaned up on one arm and whispered through a wicked giggle, "Well, she can't have children. That's a fact. But it doesn't appear to stop him from fathering babies!''

Mrs. Quinlan appeared shocked. "Why, Suzanne,

whatever do you mean?"

There were nervous whispers and giggles all through the room. Amber wondered how she could have been so sleepy a short time ago and be so wide awake and tense now. She tried to remember to keep the branch moving though she didn't believe it was doing anything to cool the room. She strained with every ounce of her being to hear the whispers as the gossipers lowered their voices.

"All's you need to do is look around you a bit," whispered the blonde. "The nigger girl a fannin' us could pass for the little princess' twin."

The mousey one joined in. "She's Lorena's child. You remember? The pretty wench? Yes, come to think of it, I 'member when Lorena was his own personal maid - and I do mean personal."

All the ladies giggled and the room began to swim before Amber. She guessed that down deep she'd known for some time now that Big Massa must be her Daddy. But to know that everyone else also knew it was too much to bear. She tried to keep the fan moving though she felt as if she would pass out momentarily. She wiped the sweat from her brow and blinked the tears away.

Then the hateful Mrs. Quinlan spoke. "Well, ladies, I've just been holdin' my peace. 'Cause you see, I didn't know what you all knew. And far be it from me to be a tale-bearer. But since you all seem to know about his carousin' around, I may as well tell all! My John was a-talkin' to 'his highness' himself the other day and says my John, 'You know, Luther, that slave child of Lorena's and your daughter look like twins.

Don't your missus ever ride you about it?' And Luther, he says, 'Funny you should ask. The older they get, the more obvious it becomes. And the wife, well, she do be upset. Some of her relatives noticed it at Christmas. So now she is all over me to do something about it. What? I says. And she says, Sell her. So I says, Okay, I'll ask my friend, John. But she says, Oh, no, don't you be selling her to any of our neighbors. I never want to lay eyes on her again!' So Luther, he tells my John, and mind you, I got it straight, that as soon as his little girl's birthday barbecue is over, he's gonna sell that yeller gal as far away as he can.'' This whole narrative was spoken in a stage whisper that Amber could not possibly have missed.

"I has ta think! I has ta think! Don't faint . . . Don't faint!" Amber kept repeating these things to herself in perfect rhythm to the fan.

Finally, though none of the ladies in Amber's room had slept a wink, a bell sounded out by the lawn which signalled that nap time was over. Amber and Lucy stood the fans in the corner and methodically relaced girdles, rebuttoned dresses, and recombed curls. The ladies filed past the girls and down the great steps. When they ran into Big Missy on the landing, they said things like, "We were chatting about what a wonderful party this is," and "We rested beautifully. There was a lovely breeze."

"Liars!" hissed Amber as she opened the blinds and tidied the beds.

Lucy had never been close to Amber, but she put her arm around the child's shoulders. "Don' pay them no mind. They's hateful old biddies. And what they said, why, they's no truf in it at all!''

But Amber looked straight into Lucy's eyes. And they both knew. Lucy dropped her head and said, ''We best go to de kitchen. They prob'ly needs all the help they . . .''

Amber ran past her nearly knocking her down in the process. ''I gots ta think! I gots ta think!'' she mumbled.

She ran down the back stairs and out the kitchen dog trot door. She ran by instinct, around the back of the house and along the edge of the woods. Carefully she had avoided contact with any of the white folks. Her tears came so fast she couldn't see. Her body was overcome by great heaving sobs. She ran the full length of the slave quarters and there was nowhere else to run without going into the woods. So she shoved her way into the last cabin in the quarters. No one had lived there for several years and it was in a sorrier state than most of the cabins. Throwing herself across the tiny cot in the corner, Amber laid there until the sobbing finally subsided. A rat scurried across the floor and Amber stifled a scream. Her head was reeling and her arms ached from the long afternoon of fanning. She kept repeating over and over, ''Jesus, help me. I gots ta think.'' But her body's needs took over and she fell into an exhausted sleep.

Young Missy's party had broken up and the guests were gone long before Massa's family had even noticed the missing slave girl. Satin had been dressed in red livery that day, helping to escort the guests to their waiting carriages. As the last guests left, Young Missy had shouted from the side veranda.

"You there, Satin. What's become of that lazy sister of yours? I want to get out of my party dress before I curry my new ponies. And she's nowhere to be found. Lucy said she saw her heading toward your Mama's place with her hand over her mouth a while ago. Go fetch her for me."

Satin dropped his head, mumbled "Yes, ma'am," and ran for the quarters. But Lorena hadn't seen Amber. Neither had anyone else. All the slaves who weren't otherwise occupied began to go from hut to hut in search of the missing girl.

Fortunately it was Satin who shoved open the door of the long-empty cabin and found the sleeping girl. Aggravated and a bit fearful as to the consequences of his sister's stupidity, he shook her brusquely and whispered hoarsely.

"Amber, what you be doin' chile? You's prob'ly in big trouble. Young Missy wants you. Get up and . . ." But he stopped abruptly for Amber had begun to cry. Always softhearted where his sister was concerned, he dropped down in front of her and took her hands in his. "What is it, sweetie? Tell Satin."

"I heard the womens talkin'. I was fannin' them during they's nap." A spasm of choking overtook the girl. Satin rubbed her back and said, "Easy. Easy."

Sobbing quietly between words she choked out, "They said Big Massa is my real daddy and they . . ."

"You didn't know, did you, Amber?" The brother shook his head sadly. "Mama was gwine tell you soon."

"Oh, that part. Well, it . . . was a surprise . . . but it wasn't. You know, Satin, I think down deep I've known it for a long time. I mean, you're so black and I's nearly white. And even I kin see how much I 'sembles Young Missy. But Satin, those women said hateful stuff about Mama and . . .''

Satin stood and rammed his hand against the tumble-down shack's wall so hard it shuddered. "Amber, you listen to me. Our Mama never did nothin' wrong. She didn't have no choice. She's . . . we's all . . . nothin' but slaves!''

Now Amber had control of herself and was standing up brushing the cobwebs from her hair and dress. "You don't have to convince me. But listen, those women said Big Massa has promised Big Missy that he's gonna . . . gonna sell me off far away!'' Her voice broke again and the tears poured forth. "Satin, I is so scared. What is I gwine do?''

Shoving her out the door Satin reasoned, "First we tell Mama.'' So the two walked across the rear lot in the gathering gloom and sneaked in the back door of their mother's cabin.

"Lawd, be praised,'' Lorena sighed as she rose stiffly from her knees. There were tears on her face and her bed was rumpled where she'd knelt petitioning the Lord for her daughter. "Amber, honey,'' she continued, "Where's you been? Young Missy been havin' a fit. You'd best . . .''

But her son interrupted. "Mama, I's been thinkin'. I think you best let me run and tell Young Missy some sort of lie. Amber's in no condition to work. This chile is heart sick clean through. Mama, she heard someone say they's gwine sell her far off on account of Big Missy found out about who she Daddy is.''

Lorena collapsed onto the stool by the table. "Oh, Lawsy, what we gwine do?"

The son realized that it was time for him to be the man in the family and take charge. "First, I's gwine go tell Young Missy that Amber took off terrible sick. I'll says she's a-heavin' and such. I'll get 'em all convinced she'd best stay away from Young Missy lest she cotch sumpin. In de meantimes, Mama, you clean up Amber and make her eat sumpin. I'll be right back."

As he took off for the house at a run, he heard Lorena say, "Amber, honey. I's been meanin' to tell you 'bout this for a time and a time."

Satin smiled to himself. He knew it had been a terrible shock to Amber but 'twasn't nothing they couldn't handle. Working together as a family, they'd think of something. But for now his task was to tell Young Missy a mighty convincing lie.

"Lawd, does I dare to ask you to help me with this? Is this anything like the time in the Old Testament that Brother Josiah told about in church? When the harlot, Rahab, lied about hiding the spies? Lawd, I doesn't know . . . and I doesn't have time to ask no one, so please, Lawd, just hep me and guide us. Fo' Jesus' sake. Amen."

He ran into the big house yelling, "Young Missy. Young Missy!"

Chapter Thirteen

While Amber, Lorena and Satin tried to decide what
they should do, back in Hannah's cabin on the banks of
the Ohio River, Constance explained to the uninformed
Prudy that while many masters in the southern states
treated their darky slaves well, there were many who
didn't. "Some of them beat them just like animals. And
if they need money, sometimes they sell them with
never a thought as to dividing up families. So, many of
the slaves have begun to run away. They used to want
to go back to Africa, their homeland. But now many of
them just choose to run north to freedom."

Prudy didn't want her friend to think she was completely stupid on the subject. "I know there are lots of
folks getting upset about slavery. I know Ohio is a free
state, so I guess if any of them run away, they'd be free
as soon as they crossed the river, right?"

"Well, sort of. Thee sees there are men called
bounty hunters that the southern plantation owners hire
to hunt down the ones who run. In fact, a bounty hunter
somewhere started the name. When he couldn't find a
slave that had escaped, he said it was as if he escaped on
some underground railroad. So, even though they are
actually free as soon as they cross the Ohio, most of 'em

keep right on runnin' north until they get to Canada. That's a different country and nobody cooperates with the bounty hunters there.''

"You mean people around here help the bounty hunters?" Prudy asked incredulously.

"Oh, yes. Thee doesn't know who thee can trust. That's why the railroad is such a big important secret. Pru, my Mamma would skin me alive if she knew I was tellin' thee.''

"I'll never tell," promised her friend. "Where are the tracks? Does it start way down south somewhere?"

Constance giggled involuntarily but immediately sobered when she saw the hurt look on her friend's face. "I'm sorry. I asked the same questions last year when I found out. There isn't really a railroad at all. It's just sort of a code name or secret term for the way north.''

"But if there's no track to follow, don't the people get lost?''

"Well, not as long as they always head north. It's a clear night. Come over to the window. I'll show thee something.''

Pulling robes on over their nighties, the two stumbled to the big front window. "See that shape in the stars up there? There's three stars in the handle and then four that form like a cup.''

"Oh, Truth told us in school that they call that the big dipper. But what's that got to do with anything?''

"The two stars at the front of the cup part point directly at the North Star. If the slaves always keep the North Star in sight and head towards it, then they know they're going the right direction.''

"Let's get back to the fire. It's turnin' off chilly," Prudy complained.

"The negroes call the big dipper the drinking gourd. They think God put it in the sky especially to lead them to freedom. They say it's a wonder how the drinkin' gourd always points them to the North Star."

"The North Star - that's the name of Captain Phil's boat!" Prudy exclaimed.

"Shhh. Thy Grandmother might hear."

"Oh, she's asleep. And, anyway, she's getting deaf."

"Well, thou art catching on fast. Captain Phil is a conductor on this pretend Underground Railroad. His boat goes way down south on the Kanawha and brings slaves up north. He hides them in all sorts of places on the boat. Down deep in the hold. Sometimes even in big barrels right in plain view."

Prudy was so astounded she couldn't speak.

"So that night that thee talked about when someone knocked on thy door and said, 'A friend with friends' and then the Captin left . . .''

"Whoa! Slow down. We're going too fast. Are you saying that there was a 'friend' standing right on my porch with escaping slaves and my Papa sent them on their way on the Captain's boat? Then that means my Papa is . . ." She was unable to finish the fearful sentence.

"Yes, he must be a conductor on the railroad, too! Hast thou ever heard him say anything about freight or shipping dry goods or hardware anywhere?"

"No, why? Are those special words too?"

"Yes. As I understand it, freight means people to

underground railroaders. Could be men and women, even children. If they talk specifically of dry goods, it means women. And hardware stands for men.''

"Wait a minute! Ooh, this is too scary. But I just remembered. When I came to visit last week I told Papa that I wanted to wait and come on the North Star. He said, 'No, Captain Phil has a large freight order to be delivered.' Oh, and I just remembered - he told me to tell Uncle Willy that likely there'd be some dry goods in this shipment for him. Connie, what'll we do? I never remembered to give him the message!"

The room was completely still for a few minutes save the crackling from the fire and the ticking of Cowma's big clock.

"Try not to worry. Thee'll just have to tell Willy tomorrow. Likely it didn't hurt anything that thee forgot. Sometimes it takes a long time to get the slave people together and ready to come. 'Sides, we haven't seen hide nor hair of Captain Phil or his boat so likely they're just not here yet."

Prudy wiped tears from her eyes. "Oh, if I thought I'd hurt some poor negro's chance for freedom! But wait, Con. This must mean my Great-Uncle Willy's involved."

Connie nodded. "Didn't thee wonder why I punched thee on the way to the outhouse tonight? Thy Grandmother had just said she noticed a candle in the front window of Willy and Nancy's house. She said it never used to be there."

"So?"

"A candle in a window facing south is another sign of the railroad. Thy uncle is surely a conductor on the same line as thy Papa and Captain Phil and . . ." After a long pause Prudy finished the sentence.

"Your Mama! You said down on the beach that my Papa and your Mama were both in it. But what do you mean 'same line'? And what about your Papa?"

"Well, there are several lines of this great big railroad system. I know 'cause we've moved three times that I can remember, so this is the third line that we've lived on. But they all lead to the same place - the north - and Canada. All the lines go north from here. When they get clear to the northern edge of Ohio the slaves go on a big boat called the Mayflower across a big lake into Canada. Isn't it all just wonderful?" Now that the telling of the wonderful secret was nearing an end, Constance stifled a yawn.

"No, no, don't get sleepy," begged Prudence. "I have so many questions! Isn't it all dangerous?"

"Of course it is. Some of our neighbors back in Virginia were caught helping a slave to escape. The slaveholders in the area got all upset. They came and hung the man who helped."

"Hung him?" Prudy nearly shouted. "Oh, Connie, at first I thought it was exciting and fun. But now I'm getting scared. What would happen if my Papa . . . or Uncle Willy . . ."

"How dost thee think I feel? It's my Mama who is the conductor at our station. Remember what I said the other day about the statue that holds a flag only when my Papa is away? Since he's a Federal Judge, the only time it is safe for any slaves to come through our house is when he is away. See, he'd have to uphold the law and send them back to their masters if he knew."

"Do you really think he doesn't know anything about it?"

"Well, I'm not sure. It seems queer to me that he always sends word to Mama when he'll be back. My oldest brother says he knows and that is his way of warning her to get them out of the house."

"Where do you hide the slaves?"

"I'll show thee on Monday."

"Are there other special words that I need to listen for?"

"No, I think I've told thee just about all the signs I know. A good conductor bringing slaves will always knock three times and then wait to be acknowledged. That is when they say the line about friends."

"But lots of the people involved aren't of your religion. Why do they call themselves friends?"

"No, they mean friends of the colored people, I suppose. This is much bigger than religion though, Prudy. People of all walks of life and different religions unite together to bring people to freedom. On the other hand, there are good people in all sorts of religions that think the whole railroad is sinful."

"How could they?" Prudy asked, outraged. "Surely Jesus wanted everyone to be free whether they were black or white. The verse I learned for Sunday School this week is, *Ye shall know the truth and the truth shall make you free.*"

"I agree with thee," whispered Connie, patting her friend's arm, "Thee's got to keep thy voice down. But there are some as says God ordained for black people to be slaves. My Mama had me memorize a verse a long time ago to settle it in my mind. It's Deuteronomy

23:15.''

"What's it say?"

Thou shalt not deliver unto his master the servant which is escaped from his master unto thee.

"I want to memorize that verse too, Constance. Remind me of it in the morning."

"Speaking of morning, it will be here long before we're ready. And we're gonna have a time tryin' to stay awake in church. Best we go to sleep now."

"I guess you're right. Oh, Constance, how will I ever sleep again? I'm so scared."

"Thee has to get over the scared part and just be proud that thy family's involved like I am."

"How can you not be scared?"

"Well, I don't know what thee calls it in thy religion. We Quakers do what we call 'centering down.' We look deep within ourselves to find peace, even when the world around us isn't peaceful. There can be peace deep inside."

"The kind only God can give. I guess I'll have to do what another Sunday School verse said, *Casting all your cares on him, for He careth for you.* I'll just give these cares to Jesus. Goodnight, Constance."

The girls hugged sweetly and Constance said, "Goodnight."

All had been quiet for several minutes when Prudy sleepily asked, "But what if it's a cloudy night?"

"What?" asked Constance, just on the edge of sleep.

"How can they always go north if it's a cloudy night? Or even in the daytime?"

Constance flopped over on her back. Without opening her eyes she mumbled, "Moss on trees."

Now it was Prudy's turn to ask the one-word question. "What?"

"Moss on trees. Always grows on the north side."

"Oh! Well, goodnight again."

A soft snore was her only reply.

Chapter Fourteen

The next morning dawned bright and clear. Constance had never been to Sunday School or any church other than the Quaker Friends services. Her eyes shone with excitement as Hannah plaited her waist-length hair into braids.

"Stand still, child. You're going to fly apart," she admonished.

"Thee just can't imagine how excited I am. Prudy, art thou just about ready to go? I can't wait to get there and see all the other children and sing songs and . . ."

"Don't they do any of those things at your church?" asked the incredulous Prudy.

Not wanting to be disloyal, Constance looked confused. "Well, no, there isn't anything special for children. And we don't sing very much. But still and all, I like our services. Thee would too if thee ever . . ."

Hannah was thankful for the wagon wheels they heard in the back yard that interrupted a tense moment for Constance. "Poor child," Hannah mumbled and then chuckled to herself at the incongruity. Constance was a rich child in comparison to Prudy. But all Hannah could see at the moment was that the child appeared to be living an extremely sheltered life. She hoped the services they were about to attend would not confuse Connie.

The two girls hopped up into the back of the springboard wagon while Willy helped his mother up and got her settled on the seat next to Nancy who offered Diggy to his Grandmother's willing arms.

Willy was climbing back up to his seat when Constance nudged Prudy. "Thee mustn't forget again."

As the wagon began to roll, Prudy cleared her throat and began. "Uncle Willy, I forgot to give you a message from my Papa."

Willy's back stiffened and he cast a sidelong glance at Nancy. "What is it, Pru?"

"Umm, let me see. He said to tell you that Captain Phil would be coming upriver with the North Star e'er long and it would have a large shipment of freight - and likely there'll be some dry goods in it for you." Prudy hoped that she had made her voice sound extremely casual. Evidently she succeeded because Hannah didn't seem to notice the highly charged atmosphere that suddenly prevailed.

"Oh, I didn't know you'd ordered dry goods, son."

Willy sort of choked. Nancy patted him on the back and said, "Somethin' go down the wrong pipe, husband?" Offhandedly she answered Hannah's question. "Baby Diggy is growing so fast. I asked Phil to bring me every soft material he could find to make him some larger gowns and things. Likely that's what the shipment will be." Turning to Prudy, she continued, "I'm so glad you remembered to tell us. We'll have to be watching for the North Star. If your Papa e'er sends us another message through you, make sure you tell us as soon as you arrive."

"I'm sorry, Aunt Nancy." Prudy's eyes were ready
to overflow.

Finally regaining his composure, Willy turned
around and tweaked her nose. "There's no harm, child.
Now, let's hear your memory verse."

Soon they pulled into the church yard. The children
all filed into the basement of the austere white building.
A lady was standing in front of the room directing that
the smallest children should sit on the first backless
bench and so forth. Prudy and Constance found a spot
at the end of the fourth bench just as the lady asked
them all to bow their heads for prayer.

Later that day as they all sat at Hannah's kitchen
table still licking their lips after a delicious boiled
dinner followed by pumpkin pie, Nancy questioned the
little guest.

"Connie, what did you think of our church?"

The little girl paused. "I liked it. It was really - fun.
But . . . well, is it always so . . . so noisy?"

Prudy stared open-mouthed. "Noisy? I think it is so
quiet here at Cowma's church! At our church down at
Burning Springs we have men playing instruments
when we sing: a mandolin and a jew's harp and when
Brother Niles can make it, we have a guitar!"

Connie spoke again. "At my church we don't even
sing. Let alone have instruments. We just sit in silence
most of the time. That's why thy service seemed so -
well, strange to me. Every now and then a man will
share what God has told him. But it's usually just a few
sentences followed by more silence. Thy reverend,
Swank, is it? - he certainly must have had God tell him

a lot this day. I thought he would never stop talking.''

Willy chuckled. ''I'm certain our way of worship seems as odd to you as yours would to us. But, did you understand it? Get anything out of it?''

As an elder in the church, Willy was genuinely concerned that the gospel be very pure and simply put forth from their pulpit.

''Oh, yes, sir. I had heard the story of Jesus looking for the lost sheep before. Mama and Papa read the Bible to us each evening and we talk about what we read and then Papa prays aloud.''

''And what did you think of Sunday School?'' Hannah asked. The ladies of the church took turns teaching the children. Today the lady in charge was the best of the lot to Hannah's way of thinking.

''It was very - nice,'' Constance wanted to say the right thing. ''I've ne'er heard children sing so loudly. But I enjoyed the story of Queen Esther.''

Prudy interrupted, ''Teacher said Esther was very brave 'cause when she went in to see the King, he could have killed her. She said, 'If I perish, I perish.' Winning freedom for her people was awful important to her.''

''Ought to be for everyone,'' Willy said fervently. ''Nancy, as soon as you finish helpin' Mama with the dishes, we best take Diggy home for his nap.''

''You children run on. Prudy and Connie can help me.''

So goodbyes were said and the clean-up was begun.

Late that afternoon the two girls sat under a large chestnut tree about half-way down the path to the river making daisy chains of dandelion stems. Constance was telling Prudy more tales of the Underground Railroad as they worked.

"Thee are certain thy grandmother can't hear us?" the worried visitor asked for what seemed the hundredth time to Prudy.

"Will you relax? As long as you're speaking in that heavy whisper of yours, she couldn't even hear us if we were in the same room. And besides, you saw her fall asleep in her rocking chair same as I did. There's no way she could hear us at this distance from the house. Go on with the story," Prudy implored.

"Well, like I was saying, it can be a fearsome business. At our old house down in Virginia just afore we moved here, there was an incident!" Now that Constance was sure no one could hear, she warmed to the storytelling like a puppy would to a dish of fresh cream.

"An incident?" Prudy's large eyes were like saucers in her face and she glanced over her shoulder at Cowma's house involuntarily. Laying aside all pretense of working on the daisy chain, she flopped on her stomach with chin in hands only inches from where the little Quaker girl's legs were crossed Indian fashion. "Do tell, Con!"

"We lived near a settlement of German-speaking Mennonites. They had left Germany because they weren't allowed to practice their religion as they wanted. So naturally they were sympathetic to the plight of the Negro slaves. They weren't really a part of the railroad. 'Twas just that they helped move the people along whenever my father was at home and our station was closed."

"What happened? What was the incident?" Prudy repeated the barely familiar word with a sense of awe.

"Mama always blamed herself for not thinking to tell the people what to be careful of. But one would have thought they would think . . ."

"Constance Woodcutter, please! What happened?" Prudy's patience grew thin as she noticed the dropping sun's rays. Her grandmother would likely awaken at any moment.

"All right. Here it is. This German family had only sons. A group of slaves, two women, two boys, and a little girl, came travelling together. The women were sisters. And all three children belonged to Dilcy, the one with golden skin. Their master had lost money, gambling in a wicked card game. So he said he was going to sell the two boys down into the deep south to raise money. Dilcy knew she'd never see her sons again if that happened. So they all ran. Oh, they'd had a frightful time of it already by the time they reached our home. As usual my brother watched carefully because Papa was home. One night he heard a wild bird call of some type and left. Thee understands? 'Twas the Negro's way of asking where they should go since the little livery boy statue did not hold the flag."

She paused to make sure Prudy was following her. At a nod from her listener, she continued.

"Darrell directed them to the Mennonite town as always. The next day a horrible, mean sheriff pounded on our door. Papa answered. 'Sir, we-uns is a-huntin' a bunch of niggers what's runned away. We's got reason to believe they are in this area.' My Papa got righteously angry, least that's what Mama always calls it when his nostrils flare and his face gets red and he yells. Well, he shouted, 'Sir, I am a Federal Judge. Surely you can't be accusing me of helping the poor Negroes.'''

'''Mayhap not you, Sir. But there's talk in town that your wife is a Quaker who . . .' He never finished that sentence for my Mama walked out from behind the door and smiled ever so sweet. She said, 'It is true what thou sayest, sir. I am a Quaker. But my husband being a judge, there's no way I could help those people to escape. Can I get thee some tea?' The sheriff got all embarrassed and said to Papa, 'No, no, tell your wife we cannot accept her offer. But answer me this, Judge Woodcutter. Do you know the German-speaking folk out north of here?'''

'''Yes, indeed. They are fine neighbors. They keep to themselves mostly. But, because I speak a bit of German, I help them out betimes. Like at the store in town. What about them?'''

'''The family in the first house in their little settlement. The one with the bright red shutters at every window? Be ya knowin' them?'''

"Papa answered straight out. 'Surely do. That would be the Brenneman farm. Fine family.'''

'''How many would you say in the family?' the nasty sheriff asked, and his beady little eyes got all squinty as he asked."

'''Man, woman, and three near-grown boys. Why?' Papa asked."

"But by then the sheriff was chuckling and running to his horse. There was a group of men on horses. 'Thanks, Judge. Ya've been a big help. A mighty big help!' he shouted as they rode north. Oh Prudy, there was no way my Papa could know that the little Mennonite lady, wanting to be good to the slaves, had washed all their clothes for them. The sheriff had noticed when he had come by their house that there was a little girl's dress and underslip hanging on the line. The next thing we knew, they had captured all five of the slaves and burned down the little Mennonite family's house and barn. Prudy, I saw them making those slaves walk back to their owners. They had chains around their ankles and their hands tied to a big stick behind their backs. The little girl wasn't even half as big as you or me!''

Connie wiped tears from her eyes as she remembered the vivid scene which was forever etched on her mind.

"Slavery really is hateful. It must be stopped!'' Prudy exploded. More quietly she asked, "Did they kill the German-speaking people?''

"No, but they beat up the oldest son till he exposed where the slaves were hiding. Some neighbors came out to help them, but the sheriff and his posse turned guns on all of them.''

"Was there a battle?''

"No, Mennonites are like the people of my religion, Prudy. They don't believe in fighting or killing. They didn't even own any guns. So they had to just stand there and watch the Brenneman farm burn to the ground. 'Cause the gunmen would've shot them if they'd tried to stop it.''

"What happened to the family? Where did they live?''

"I'm not sure because very soon after the incident

my family moved. That's another reason Darrell and I
think Papa knows about Mama's station. We move so
often.''

Squeezing her hand, Prudence said, ''Oh, I hope you
don't have to move from here. You're my bestest friend
ever.''

Just then Hannah called the girls to come into the
house. Their last night together seemed to go all too
quickly. After a pick-up supper, they told stories and
sang songs. Hannah even taught them a rhyming game
which she'd learned years ago to help her make the
switch from speaking German to English. All too soon
Hannah indicated that it was time for two adventurous
young ladies to spread their pallets by the fire.

The house had been quiet for some time when Prudy
reached over and tapped Connie's shoulder.

''Con, are you awake?''

''I am now,'' her friend grumbled. ''What dost thee
want?''

''When you moved away, what happened to the
slaves then? Who helped?''

Immediately understanding that her friend was
thinking of the incident, she replied, ''Mama and
Darrell went to say goodbye to the Germans. So I can
only suppose they arranged for a new station. Probably
taught them things to be careful about. We'd better go
to sleep.''

''Where do you hide them in your new house?''

''There's a totally sealed-off room. The only way to
get to it is to climb through the attic. If we get a chance,
I'll show it to thee tomorrow.''

Settling down, Prudy shivered involuntarily.

"It's dangerous, isn't it?"

"Fearsome dangerous. But somebody's got to do it," responded her sleepy companion.

Chapter Fifteen

The next several months passed by very quickly. Prudy had to end her visit to Cowma and go back home for school. In years to come, the family would remember this peaceful time and refer to it as "the calm before the storm."

They were half-way through the school term at Burning Springs when it became apparent that this would be Truth's last year to teach. In the early days it was just that she seemed grouchier than usual. Then she began having the oldest girl watch the classroom periodically so she could go to the outhouse. She often returned from these trips white and a little shaky. As the months progressed and her clothes grew tighter, even the smallest children were heard to whisper, "Teacher's in the family way."

A special meeting was held by the school board to discuss the dilemma.

"Well, I never! In my day such things were never spoken of openly. And from the time that a woman starts to show, she shouldn't be seen."

"Oh, now, Harriet, let's be reasonable. After all, this is 1822 and we are not the Puritans. The children need an education."

"Forevermore, Mr. Wilson! What can you be thinking of? It's not decent, I tell you. I agree with Harriet. The school should be closed."

"But listen, folks. These aren't stupid city children. They've all seen and helped farm animals be birthed. And most all of 'em has younger siblings. I say we let Truth keep teachin' right up till her time comes."

At this suggestion, Harriet swooned. They grabbed the smelling salts from her reticule and she revived quickly. Just in time to hear her own husband, of all people, arguing on the opposite side of the issue from herself.

"Isn't the education of the children what's most important? Truth Longtree is the only qualified teacher within miles and miles. And it's not like she wouldn't behave herself with the proper amount of decorum. She can hide her condition in long Mother Hubbards. I say we let her teach."

When Harriet was fully revived, she glared at her balding little husband and shouted, "Let us vote. That's the only fair way to handle such an important issue as this."

When the vote was taken, reason won out over Victorian principles. School was allowed to continue. The end-of-school picnic was held on May first.

On May third, Truth gave birth to a bouncing, black-haired, black-eyed son. They named him William after the great-great-grandfather he would never meet on earth and Robert after his father.

"What's this?" asked Rev. Swank when he was told. "A Stivers baby with just a normal name?"

Hannah chuckled. "True wrote that she just couldn't

come up with a quality for a name. And besides, she said, 'The very name William is the embodiment of all I want my baby to be. If he's half the man his great-great-grandfather was, I'll be pleased.'" Hannah's voice broke for a minute. Then she went on. "She also said in the letter that they are going to call him Will - never Bill! I'm to go down for his christening, Reverend, did you know? Why, if anyone would have e'er told me that I'd live to see great-great-grandchildren, I'd have said they were daft!"

"The North Star is anchored down near the town center. By Judge Woodcutter's home. Will you be going south on that then?" the parson asked.

"Yes, we are to sail the day after tomorrow. Willy and Nancy were going to go too, but she's not feeling pert these days, so I don't know."

"I must be off, Mrs. Stivers. It's always good to visit with you. Maybe I'll run up the hill and see Nancy. Diggy is turning into quite a little man, isn't he?"

Hannah enjoyed visiting with the minister but, truly, she was glad to see him go. Lately, if she didn't take a nap in the afternoon, she could hardly function.

Instead of improving, Nancy's condition worsened. Her symptoms were so vague it was hard to get an accurate diagnosis. But on the night before Hannah left for Burning Springs, Willy knocked at the door. In fact, he had to pound quite hard to make his mother hear.

"Just a minute, I'm coming," she shouted as she lit the lamp from her bedside table. Pulling a shawl about her shoulders, Hannah tried in vain to estimate what time it was. She knew it must be the middle of the night because she had been sleeping so soundly.

"Willy!" she exclaimed as she closed the door behind him. "What is it, son? You're white as a sheet."

"Mama, Nancy's bleeding! I've got to go to town for the doctor. Can you come up and stay with . . ."

Hannah never heard the rest of the question for she was in her room pulling on her stockings and shoes. Willy held her arm and thanked God she was so close as he led her up the hill to his house. He went inside with Hannah just long enough to check on Nancy, then ran to the barn to prepare for his fast ride into town. Thankfully, Dignity was sleeping soundly.

The sun was rising over the springhouse roof when the doctor emerged from Nancy's room. He sat down dejectedly at the kitchen table and took the cup of strong, hot coffee Hannah offered with a wan smile.

"'Twas quite a messy affair, Mrs. Stivers. Willy, from what I can gather it looks to me as though your wife had been expecting . . . twins, or maybe triplets. She wasn't very far along so it's hard to be certain. But something went wrong. I'm sorry."

Willy's hands were trembling. "Sorry?" he croaked. "Do you mean - is Nancy . . ."

"Oh, no, Nancy's fine. In fact, I s'pect she'll be fit as a fiddle in just a few days. But - she lost the babies, and Willy, - well, I don't think you should try to have any more children. It's just . . . not wise . . . do you understand, son?"

Willy was crying but Hannah could tell they were tears of relief and joy that Nancy was alive and going to be all right.

"Can I see her?" he begged and the doctor went into the bedroom with him.

Hannah began to prepare a big batch of mush and fry some fresh side meat for their breakfast. As she stood over the stove, her own tears caused little splatters in the hot grease.

"Lord," she prayed, "I thank you for bringing Nancy safely through. Why, Jesus, I never realized until just this moment how close I feel to her. I don't know who ever invented the term 'in-law.' 'Cause Nancy feels as close to me as a real blood daughter. I love her nigh as much as Libby. And I sure am grateful that you brought her through this. And, God, when it truly hits her that she was expectin' babies - I don't think she even knew - and when she realizes she lost 'em . . . well, comfort her. Don't let her and Willy mourn what might have been. Just let 'em love Diggy more and enjoy him."

The fresh side was done and the mush just beginning to brown a little as the doctor and Willy emerged from the bedroom.

"How is she?" Hannah asked.

"She just fell asleep," was the response.

"Doctor, can you take breakfast with us?" Hannah asked as the old gentleman was putting on his hat.

"No, my office opens in just a little over an hour, and I want to call on the Le Clerque's before that. Their little Pierre is mighty sick with the measles."

"Oh, I see. Well, then, can you do us a favor? I need to get a message to Captain Philip Woodcutter of the packet boat, the North Star. I was to take a voyage south with him today but, under the circumstances, I'll . . ."

"No, Mother. We've already discussed it." Willy interrupted. "All Nancy needs is rest and some warm nourishing soups and broths for the next few days. I can stay here and care for her. The way you can be the biggest help to us - and the doctor agrees - would be to go on your trip.''

Hannah was shaking her head until Willy added, ''And take Diggy with you.''

Now the old woman was truly befuddled. ''Diggy! On the boat! Oh, my, I don't know if I could handle him.'' Her eyes filled with tears. ''Such a responsibility. I don't know.''

The doctor patted her arm. ''Mrs. Stivers, Nancy was completely at peace with the idea of you taking the little guy to Burning Springs with you. It would be the best way on earth you could help them . . . to get him out from under foot so Nancy can rest and get her strength back. She's really lost a lot of blood and been through quite an ordeal.''

''Of course I want to help, but . . .'' Hannah hesitated.

''I know. Whyn't we ask the Woodcutters if Miss Constance could travel with you? She could help to occupy Diggy and get to visit Prudy at the same time.''

At this suggestion Hannah brightened. ''Why, yes. Connie would be a help. But would it be fair to Dilly for us to show up unannounced with Connie and Diggy?''

''Mama, she was expecting Nancy and me and Dig. And anyway, you know Dilly. She's as calm as the Kanawha River. She rolls with the flow.''

And so it was that later that afternoon Captain Phil docked the North Star right at the edge of Hannah's walk and escorted Mrs. Stivers aboard. He carried Dignity until he got into the driver's shanty, where they joined a very excited Connie.

"Oh, Mrs. Stivers, I still can hardly believe that I get to go. We had lots of extra work to do, what with Papa away and the big shipment that Captain Phil brought." Here the Captain threw her a warning glance and shook his head sternly behind Hannah's head. The child tried to cover her near-mistake. "But Mama said I was needed to help with darling little Dignity." With this she lifted the toddler onto her lap and began to sing a counting song merrily.

The Captain went ashore to confer with Willy for several moments and then, at last, they were on their way.

Four days later the visit was history. True's baby, Will, had cried vehemently all through the christening ceremony, stopping only when rocked by Hannah. Dignity had been almost angelic during the trip. The only anxious moment had been on the second night at bedtime when he began to whimper, "I want my Mama." Connie came to the rescue with the suggestion that if he were allowed to hold one of the new puppies from the barn until he fell asleep, perhaps he would forget being homesick. It worked like a charm. True to Willy's prediction, Dilly had been delighted to help with Diggy and had also been persuaded to allow Prudy to return home with her beloved Cowma. The pretense was that she could help with Diggy and speed Nancy's recovery. But the actual fact, as everyone knew, was that two young ladies who were best friends yearned for more time together.

Captain Phil seemed tense on the return trip. There were only two other passengers on the boat, a lady from the deep south and her colored maid. The lady was covered from head to foot in widow's weeds, as the mourning garments had begun to be called. Hannah had never seen such a heavy material used for the veil of a hat. She had no clue as to the age of the widow. It must have been a recent death, though, for the woman kept her head down at all times and spoke not a word. Phil explained to Hannah that she was going up to northern Ohio to visit her late husband's relatives. Hannah thought she heard the widow giggle and, even more strangely, once the little maid called the widow "mama." But Hannah dismissed all thoughts of the strange woman at the joy of returning home and finding Nancy up and about.

Their homecoming had been delayed by about an hour for they needed to let the Woodcutters know they were home and get permission for Connie to stay at Hannah's. Phil had steered the North Star to the landing near the corner of the square in Gallipolis.

"Captain, look! My Papa is home!" Connie tugged urgently on Phil's waistcoat and pointed to the empty-handed statue. Was it fear that Hannah saw in her eyes? She certainly didn't appear to be glad that her father was home.

Yet in a few minutes when Little Marc carried Connie on his shoulders back to the boat, it seemed all was well.

"I'm turning into a worrier," Hannah mused.

Hannah's hearing was more acute at some times than at others. She caught bits and pieces of conversations between Prudy and Connie in the next few days that confused her. When she began to think about it, over the last couple years, she had noticed many little strange incidents. None of them by themselves seemed important. But suddenly, on this very warm night in early June, she felt an urgent need to talk to her son.

The girls were pushing little Dignity in his swing down by the barn when Hannah tapped on Willy and Nancy's kitchen door.

"Come in, Mama. I've just finished clearing the supper things away. There's still some hot coffee. Would you like a cup?"

"Sounds good." Hannah responded. "Willy, come and sit down with your mama. Or, do you have to light the candle in the south window?"

Willy stopped abruptly and stared at his mother. He was flustered. "Why, no . . . I . . ." he stammered.

"Nancy, Willy . . . suppose we be totally honest with each other for a few minutes. I've been noticing things for a long time. The candle, the North Star, Captain Phil's mysterious "mission in life," the statue at Little Marc's that doesn't hold a flag when he's at home, the order of dry goods that you ordered, the mysterious visitors in the middle of the night at Dilly's . . . suppose you just tell me what's going on, children."

During her narrative, Nancy and Willy had looked shocked and guilty at the same time, as they stared first at Hannah and then at each other.

Willy stammered, "Why, Mama . . . whatever do you mean? I don't know . . ."

Hannah smiled, knowing from their reactions that all her suspicions were correct. "Oh, come now, Willy. I may have been born at night . . . but it wasn't last night! Let's cut right to the bone. Is this house a station on what people call the Underground Railroad?''

Chapter Sixteen

"She believed me," Satin sighed as he dropped on the stool by the door of Lorena's hut. It was fully dark now and the only light in the cabin came from a stub of a candle on the table in the corner.

Amber and Lorena sat on the edge of the plank bed which was nailed to the wall. Amber's face had been scrubbed clean and Lorena was plaiting her unruly hair into tight french braids. She seemed to have regained her composure completely.

Turning her big blue eyes to her brother without turning her head away from Lorena's busy fingers, she said, "What did you tell them, brother?"

"I said how you took awful sick. I told 'em how sorry you is fer runnin' out on they party, but that you've jest been heavin' non-stop. I told 'em you didn' want Young Missy or none of they's house guests to git it is why you runned down here. An' I tol' 'em Mama says you is burnin' up with fever." Grinning at his sister, he added, "Chile, they don' want no part of you. Mama, Big Missy say I was supposed to tell you that you is relieved from you duties 'til Amber is well so's you can jest stay here and nurse her."

"There, one is done," Lorena said as she tied the end

of the shoulder-length braid with twine. "Now turn your head, Amber." Casting her eyes across at her son as she spoke, she said, "Satin, you's sure they believed it?"

"Yes, Mama. I tol' dem over and over how sorry she felt for lettin' dem down on Little Missy's birfday. An' I 'laborated on her vomitin' 'til I thought Big Missy was gwine upchuck herself." He giggled smugly. "Dey believed it all right. I's supposed to go tell dem how she is when I gits in from de fields tomorrow night."

"Ya done good, boy. With da good Lawd's help, and iffen we can git tickets to ride de Underground Train, we kin be long gone by dis time tomorrow night."

"Mama, what you sayin'?" both children responded in unison. Fear and excitement charged the room.

Lorena jerked Amber's head back as she deftly plaited the second braid. "I's been thinkin' and prayin'," she continued. "Onliest answer I kin see is to head north and git shut of this awful slavery once and fer all."

"But, Mama, iffen we gits caught . . ." the boy exclaimed.

"Shhh. Keep your voice down . . . and best you blow out the candle. We don' want the overseer a wonderin' what we's doin' so late at night. But wait now 'til I finish Amber's hair. There now, it won't be fallin' in your eyes whilst we's runnin', chile. Now, Satin. Blow out the light and the two of you sit here 'side me whilst I tell you everything I knows about the way to freedom."

Lorena spoke, barely above a whisper, long into the

night. Every so often she paused to ask the children if they were awake or if they understood exactly what she meant. Satin was astounded at her thorough knowledge of the secret system which helped the slaves to freedom.

"Where'd you learn all this?" he asked when the telling was finished.

"Oh, here and there. I guess I've known for a time and a time that as Amber grew up the day would come when we'd have to go . . . but I always hoped . . . now, Satin, are you clear in your mind as to our plan for the morning?"

"Yes'm! You'll go at first light and tell the foreman of the cotton fields that I've took fearsome sick so's they won't be huntin' for me. And I'm to go to the kitchen and tell the old cook 'bout Amber's bein' sick and Big Missy sayin' you not have to work."

"And?" the tiring mother prodded.

"And could she give me some corn pones and some beans and whatever else I sees so's you kin try to get some nourishment into my poor ailing sister."

"That's right. And ram your pockets and your shirt full of garden truck iffen nobody's lookin' around the garden. But mind you make sure ain't nobody watching!" Pausing for a moment to collect her thoughts, she heaved a big sigh. Then she continued, "Amber, honey, you got any questions?"

"No, Mama. I think I understand everything. I'm gettin' powerful sleepy."

"I know, baby. We's gonna go to sleep now. But jest make sure that you understand what to do iffen somepin unforeseen happens and we gits split up."

"Always go north by follerin' the drinkin' gourd in the sky. Stick to river beds as much as possible so's hounds cain't foller a scent. But Mama, we won't git us separated. Why, I'd be too plum scared to think of anything without you and Satin. I don' know as I'd even wanna be free without . . ."

"Hush yo' mouf, chile!" the mother sounded mad. "Freedom is the most precious thing they is. You's got ta want it more than anything in the world, Amber!"

"Yes, ma'am," mumbled the girl, half asleep.

"All right. I guess we's done all the preparin' we can. Now we's in the hands of the good Lawd in Heaven. Sleep well, my babies. Tomorrow we go."

Long after she could hear the soft even breathing of Satin and Amber, Lorena stared into the darkness and prayed.

At the first hint of gray dawn, Lorena shook Satin awake. "It's raining, boy, but maybe that's best. We's gonna have to face all sorts of elements afore this trip is through. You 'members the plan?" she whispered.

He nodded and took off for the kitchen while his mother went to see the cotton foreman. The plan worked so perfectly that it astounded them. An hour later, when the quarters were empty because everyone was at their assigned task, three figures stole quietly into the woods heading north.

They followed a stream which soon became more of a river as the rains swelled its banks. Over and over again they waded through the stream to the opposite side. On and on they walked without a word passing between them.

At one point the stream ran close to the sugar cane

fields. There was a crew of six of Massa's biggest hands breaking the cane. Satin saw them first and dove down against the bank, pulling Amber with him. Lorena squatted several feet behind them. They hardly breathed. Each one prayed. Finally the men moved to the other side of the field of cane and Satin felt it was safe for them to run past. Keeping in a crouched position, they skirted the field and headed into the deep woods on the opposite side of the stream. When they were well into a deep section of thick pine, Lorena took Satin by the shoulder.

"Best we rest and eat a little, son," she whispered.

"I didn't want to till we got off the plantation, Mama" argued the son. But one glance at Amber told him his mother was right. Her feet were torn and bleeding and her eyes told she was bone weary.

They sat on a soft carpet of pine and ate a corn pone apiece. They also ate a few bites of fatback the cook had given them thinking Lorena would use it to flavor the beans. After a carrot and some sips of cold water from the stream, Lorena instructed Amber to put her feet in the river. Tenderly, she washed the gravel from the cuts on her daughter's feet and then tore strips of her underskirt to bind them.

"Too bad you was a house nigger, Amber," joked Satin. "Me and Mama's feet is thicker than leather from all the work outside."

"Big Missy made me wear Little Missy's old shoes whenever she knew I was goin' outside. They hurt like the dickens 'cause my foot was already bigger than hers. But I kin see that my feet sho' has got soft," she grimaced as her mother tied the bandages tightly. Determined not to hold them back in any way, she jumped up. "Best be goin'!"

They plodded along methodically for another couple hours, barely daring to whisper to each other when suddenly Satin broke into a run.

"We's here! We's here!" He clapped as he spoke.

And, sure enough, just ahead was the three-foot-high stone wall that every slave on the plantation knew so well. It completely surrounded Big Massa's property. At one time or another, everyone was forced to help build or repair that hated stone wall.

As they clambered over the wall, the three fell atop each other in a blubbering heap.

"Lawd, be praised! We's on our way." Lorena swiped at a tear in her eye and Amber smiled for the first time in two days.

"Look, Mama. Mulberries," Satin exclaimed.

They feasted on the tasteless berries for a bit before moving on.

* * * * *

Back at the quarters, bedlam had broken loose. A sudden spasm of humanity had gripped Big Missy's heart, so she sent her own maid down to check on the child, Amber.

"If I'd known she was ailing, I wouldn't have used her to fan at the party," she explained to her husband. "I just want to know how she is, Luther."

Just then her maid entered the room with her head down.

"Well, speak up, Ellen. How is the child?"

"Not there, ma'am," mumbled the slave woman, hating herself for her own lack of resourcefulness.

"What did you say?" exploded the Master.

"She's not there, sir. Ain't nobody in Lorena's cabin. And ain't nobody seen any of them - Lorena or Satin or Amber - all day long."

Within moments, a thorough search had been made. The cotton foreman had been questioned. The cook had been interrogated. And the deception was discovered.

The Master was white hot! True, he had been about to sell Amber anyway. But it had been years since anyone had even attempted to escape from his domain. And now, of all people, the escapee was his own daughter! Oh, he would never claim her as such. But he knew it . . . and probably so did everyone else. It tore away at a man's pride to think his own blood would try . . . but thinking wasn't his strong point right now. He was so mad he couldn't think!

"Saddle the two fastest horses!" he shouted to the groom. "And get the overseer . . . and get the dogs!" Turning to his wife he said, "They will be found. I guarantee it!"

✳ ✳ ✳ ✳ ✳

The three slaves continued north as long as their legs would carry them. Then they rested. Now that they were off the plantation, they allowed themselves the luxury of conversation. Lorena told the children stories of escapes of long ago, both successful and unsuccessful. She repeated over and over again the signs she knew and understood of the Underground Railroad, praying as she did so that the children would remember.

The sun was beginning to set when it happened. The river was down in a small ravine at this point. The river bed was rocky. They determined the walking would be easier on the bank up the little cliff. Amber had nimbly climbed the embankment and was re-tying the bandages on her feet. Satin turned around to give Lorena a hand when the rock under her left foot rolled. With a brief shriek, Lorena tumbled backwards down the cliff landing in the sand at the bottom with a soft thud.

"Mama!" they both shouted and scrambled down the bank to her side.

The mother's face was contorted in pain and tears ran silently down her cheeks. "Clumsy old fool!" she cried and tried to smile.

At the same time they all three looked at her left ankle and their hearts sank. The jagged edge of a leg bone protruded through the skin just above her ankle.

"Oh, what's we gwine do? I don' know nothin' about settin' a broken leg. I's affeared we's done for now." Satin, who had tried so valiantly to grow up in one day, gave way to tears.

"No, son, don't. I'll be all right. Just go find me a straight piece of wood that I can make a splint with. And Amber, I know that dress is short already, but tear me some strips of cloth off of the hem."

The two children did exactly as their mother commanded. Before it was completely dark, the broken leg was set. Amber wondered if she would ever be able to forget the anguished scream which escaped her mother's lips when she held the leg tight and Satin slammed the bone back into the proper alignment. Lorena fainted at that point but a splash of cold water from the stream on her face had brought her around.

Now it was dark and the three lay huddled together at the base of a huge sycamore tree. Satin was going to the stream frequently to get colder water-soaked bandages made of his shirt to wrap around the swollen leg.

"It eases the throbbing some," Lorena said.

The steady drizzle which had plagued them all day gave way to a dazzling clear night. Lorena taught them both how to find the north star, praying they would absorb and remember the lesson. Finally they slept.

The eastern sky was just beginning to turn a faint pink when something disturbed Lorena. Shaking her head to clear it, at first she thought it was pain that brought her so wide awake. Gingerly she tried to move the splintered leg and it felt as if something exploded inside her limb. Blinking back the unshed tears, she started to pray when she heard it again. Unmistakably, from the south, came the baying of the hounds.

"Oh, no! Satin! Amber! Wake up! You've got to move on! Wake up!" Now she shouted, not caring if she was heard. The hounds were far off yet but she could tell they were coming in the right direction.

Chaos ruled for a few minutes. But she was firm and demanded that the children go on. "Freedom, Amber! That's all that matters. You and Satin must find freedom. Remember everything I's been telling you and go!"

With many tears and hugs, they were soon off. Satin had Amber's hand and she thought he would pull her arm out of the socket. They ran along the bank of the river heedless to brambles and shrubs. Branches hit Amber's arms and face so relentlessly that she closed her eyes and just concentrated on staying on her feet. The hounds' barking grew to such a din that her ears hurt from the sound. Then, suddenly, the barking ceased.

The two children stopped and stood completely silent. Arm in arm, with tears streaming down their faces, they heard this exchange between Big Massa and Lorena.

"Where are they?"

"Who you mean, Massa?"

"Lorena, don't! You and I both know who I mean!"

There was a slap and a stifled sob. Satin stiffened and Amber cried.

"I see you went and broke your leg. Well, never mind, it'll heal. You've still got lots of good years left, Lorena. Now tell me where those children are."

"Massa, I honestly don't know."

"I suppose that's true. You never did lie worth anything. But never fear. We'll find them. Lucius, put her on your horse with you. And tear that pack off her leg and give it to the dogs for scent. That's the boy's shirt, I believe."

Satin and Amber stood long enough to hear the awful scream when the hateful Lucius, the overseer, threw Lorena across his saddle. "Please, God let her pass out," Satin whispered. "Amber, listen, the only way we can make it is to split up. You run in the river bed. Stay in the water. It's flowin' real gentle now and it looks shallow. I'm takin' off across country."

"No! No!" she pleaded.

But he pushed her away. "Stay in the water. 'Member, Mama wanted you to be free so bad. Go!"

While Amber watched, Satin backtracked toward their mother for several yards before he took off across an open field, heading straight for the rising sun.

Knowing nothing else to do but to obey orders, Amber started to run in the water. Fortunately it was only a little more than ankle deep, so she gained ground quickly. The dogs were hot on her trail for a while, but then they turned to follow Satin's trail. On and on she ran, unable to think.

A shot rang out!

"No!" she cried, but forced herself to keep running. "Oh, Satin," she mumbled, "You gave your life for me . . . so's I could be free. Oh, Satin. Oh, Mama. Satin. Mama . . ." She ran in the water as long as she could. Then she slowed to a walk. It would be days later before she realized that the water was what kept the dogs off her trail. Her brother had been so wise.

And now she was on her own. She reviewed her mother's instructions carefully. Late that night she stumbled onto the porch of a house that had a lantern in the window facing south.

Chapter Seventeen

Hannah stayed later at Willy's house that night than she ever had before. Constance and Prudence brought Diggy in and put him to bed. When that task was accomplished, they plopped in chairs at the kitchen table, drank the hot cocoa Nancy made for them, and listened wide-eyed to the conversation. Willy related story after story of his involvement with the Underground Railroad. He and Nancy had opened their station about a year and a half ago. In that time, they had been able to help thirty-seven slaves on their way to freedom. Hannah's heart filled with pride when she learned that all of her family was involved.

"I don't know how many times the folks who come through here have also spent a day or two at Libby's down at Kelly's Creek and then at Dilly's in Burning Springs," said the son.

"Will would be so proud of all of you. And Duffy! Why, you are all still working to preserve his first name, Freedom!" But then the old lady's voice broke. "Willy, Nancy, why haven't you e'er included me? Am I so old - so worthless?"

Nancy sprang to her feet and ran to Hannah's side on the kitchen settee. "No, Mama! Please don't think that.

It's just that it's so dangerous. We didn't want you to get hurt somehow by becoming involved."

Hannah shook her head, still not convinced. "Even the children know about it," she said, looking at her great-granddaughter. "I just don't see why you kept it from me."

Willy responded to his mother's hurt. "Only Prudy knows. And only 'cause she's such a nosy little thing!" This was said with a playful tweak on the girl's nose.

At this Prudy joined in. "Uncle Willy's telling the truth, Cowma. Longsuffering and Truth haven't the first clue. I found out mostly 'cause of my friendship with Connie. But Papa and Captain Phil and everyone are always telling me to keep it a secret. That's the only reason I never told you."

Hannah still felt miffed that they'd run this operation right under her nose without consulting her. Or maybe her pride was hurt that she hadn't discovered it before. But, whatever she was feeling, her thirst for knowledge and adventure triumphed.

"Well, tell me more. Where do the slaves go from here and how do they get there? And, is there any way I can help?"

Into the wee hours of the morning the conversation continued. Finally, when Connie and Prudy had lain their heads on the table, Hannah declared that they must go home. Willy carried a lantern and offered his mother an arm. He waited discreetly while the three ladies used the outhouse and then escorted them to Hannah's porch.

"Still mad at me, Mama?" asked Willy at the door.

"Oh, don't be silly. I was ne'er mad. Just hurt. But

now I see 'twas only my welfare you had in mind. But please inform Captain Philip Woodcutter that if he e'er needs me or my house to join his track of this railroad, I'm ready. Goodnight, Willy.''

"Mama, that's a big relief to me. Y'see, Nancy's been wanting us to take off and go visit her kin for a long time. But we've ne'er done it 'cause whenever Judge Marc is home, we are Captain Phil's alternative house. If you'd really be willing, maybe we'll plan a trip up to see Nancy's family.''

"Go right ahead. I'm sure I could handle any emergency. Look there, the girls are asleep already. You best get home now, Willy. And Willy, I'm proud of you. Your father would be too.''

They embraced briefly and Willy headed up the hill with a light heart.

A few days later Captain Phil stopped in to see Hannah. "So, now you know!''

"Yes, and I'm not sure I should forgive you for not letting me in on this from day one,'' she teased him.

"It can be fearsome dangerous, Miss Hannah.'' Over the years of their reacquaintance, he had slipped into calling her 'Miss Hannah' as he had years ago as a suitor. "But it's so rewarding!''

He and Hannah worked out a daytime-only signal for her to use during Willy and Nancy's absence if it appeared that all was well for her to house a slave. The candle in the window was beginning to be known by all the bounty hunters, so each station was devising its own sign. They settled on a red bandanna tied around the scarecrow's neck. They also decided that the cellar was the obvious hiding place.

"Philip, do you think my Will could have known something like this would come about someday? You know, we have that secret passage from our cellar to the springhouse."

"Who's to say?" the Captain shrugged. "I just hope you never have to use that. I'd rather keep you out of this completely. Oh, by the way, Connie's mother sent word with me that she's needed back home. Some of the children have the ague, and her mother could use her help in nursing."

"Are you going up to see Willy? Would you ask him if he'd mind running her home this afternoon? He and Nancy are taking the baby and going visiting tomorrow. They plan to be gone a fortnight."

So the Captain took his leave, Connie was driven home, and by noon the next day, Hannah and Prudy were alone on the place.

❊　❊　❊　❊　❊

Amber couldn't even remember how many days she'd been on this quest for freedom. From that first night when she'd stumbled onto the porch of the only abolitionist in northern Louisiana, it had been as if an unseen hand was guiding her. Step by step she'd worked her way north, learning more at each stop along the way about this vast network of people willing to help slaves. And often, deep in the night, she heard rumblings - whispered talk about herself!

"She's whiter than some of my very own relation," one woman said.

Her husband retorted, "And that's why we's got to

keep her movin'. They say that her daddy fathered her
of a favorite slave. And he's determined to get her
back. She's got the highest price on her head. And
there's more bounty hunters after her than if she was a
queen. So, we's got to be powerful careful.''

Sometimes Amber wondered if she would ever see
daylight again. She was always told to sleep in some
windowless room in the daytime and forced to travel at
night.

In one little burg, the colored folks had faked a
funeral to get her out of town. They'd put her in a coffin
and the coffin in a hearse. About thirty mourners
followed the hearse out of town to the colored folks'
cemetery. In a cluster of trees at the edge of the cemetery, they swiftly opened the coffin and bade her to
climb onto the front seat of a spring wagon. A lady
draped her in a mourner's veil and the driver of the
wagon took off at a trot, heading north. Amber glanced
back across her shoulder just in time to see the funeral
procession heading back into town.

Two nights ago had been the worst experience yet.
Amber had never liked to be around hay. It made her
nose itch, tickled her throat, and often caused her to
sneeze. This night the lady who had been her hostess
said, ''C'mon chile. Now that you's been all fed and
got you a nice, clean, dry dress, it's time for you to
move on. Go with my man here to the barn.''

Upon entering the barn Amber saw a wagon all
hitched up and ready. The bed of the wagon had been
cleverly built so that it concealed a false bottom. The
farmer lifted a hinged lid and told her to get in and lie
still. After she did so, she heard and even felt some-

thing very heavy being stacked and dropped atop of the lid she lay under. She didn't have to wonder for long what it was. The odor of the hay permeated the air and Amber thought she would suffocate.

"Oh, Jesus, please help me. I can't breathe. My eyes are afire and it feels like my throat is closin'. Oh, Lawd, how's I gwine get through this night?"

The wagon seemed to go at a snail's pace. Many times Amber sneezed, hoping the noise of the horse would drown out the sound. Then the wagon stopped. She heard a man's voice shout.

"Where you goin', man?"

"Headin' to the market in the next town," replied her cool-headed friend.

"In the middle of the night?" the gruff voice responded.

"First one in gets the best price for their grain," the driver lied, hoping it sounded logical.

"Got a warrant here to search your wagon."

"What ya lookin' for?"

Amber couldn't hear quite so clearly now because something was being slammed down through the load of hay. It jolted the wagon bed each time it hit. Was it a rifle butt? Amber prayed that the fake floor would hold steady under the jolting. She felt a sneeze coming but stifled it with sheer will power.

"Just a little girl - ain't worth much - picture here. No, not her - a daguerreotype of a girl that could be her twin, 'cept 'course the one we're chasin' is a nigger. High price on her head. Well, iffen you do, look me up and I'll split the money with you."

The bounty hunter evidently rode away. Amber

sneezed violently!

"Bless you, little darlin'. We're almost there. From here on you're goin' up the Kanawha River."

And it was in the hay wagon with the fake floor that Amber arrived at Libby's house in Burning Springs.

Maybe allowing her to stay the extra day was a mistake. But of all the folk who'd come through Sam and Libby's house, they pitied Amber the most.

First of all, her face was swollen beyond measure with hives. Her eyes were swollen shut and her breath came in short hoarse wheezes.

When the driver deposited the hay in Sam's barn and opened the hinged lid, Libby gasped at what she saw.

"Is she blind?" she asked the driver. Then remembering her manners, she put an arm around the trembling girl.

"She weren't blind last night when I put her in here. And she didn't look like . . ."

Amber interrupted, "It's the hay. I never could abide hay."

"Lands, chile. Why didn't you speak up? I could've hauled Sam some corn just as easy." The driver was filled with remorse when the trembling child collapsed.

"Didn't hear nobody ask me," she said, then drifted off in a faint.

When she awoke she was in a world of white. The walls were white. She was tucked beneath and above white sheets in a wondrously soft feather bed. Libby had bathed her completely and pulled every last piece of straw from her hair. She could open her eyes a slit now, and it was easier to breathe.

"Drink this good, hot chicken broth, sweetheart,"

Libby pleaded. After Amber finished the cup, she pulled herself up in bed.

"Where is I at? Is this the land of freedom?" she asked.

"No, honey, but you're almost there. We've arranged for you to stay here a day or so and then you'll cross the Ohio River and you'll be free. Suppose we while away this evening by you telling me your story. Then tomorrow you can get up and move around some until Captain Phil picks you up tomorrow night to take you north."

So Amber told a spellbound Libby and incredulous Sam her story. She fought tears when she spoke of Satin's death for her freedom's sake.

"Another man died for your freedom, too, Miss Amber," Sam responded at the end of the narrative. "Jesus died on a cross many years ago so that we could be free from sin."

"Oh, yes, sir, I knows. I asked Him to be my Savior long time ago. Does you folkses know 'bout Jesus too?"

The three knelt together in prayer before retiring.

While Amber spent a happy day with Libby, the bounty hunters pressed forward. Amber helped to make bread and air the room she slept in. The hunters were now going door to door in Gallipolis, having gone past their prey in their quest for the rich reward.

At Le Clerque's Mercantile, the little Frenchman's beady eyes shone. "You'll be staying over at Our House? If I see or hear of anything strange, I'll surely let you know. What did you say my share of the bounty would be?"

Captain Phil was not surprised to find Amber at Libby's. "I've been hearing about this little lady for days. Seems half the countryside is lookin' for her. I'm afraid you're not going to like your accommodations aboard my ship, but it's the only way I know for sure is safe."

He put her into a large whisky barrel that sat beside the wheel house under cover of darkness that night. "Mind you be quiet. I'll try to let you out for a few minutes each night. But with the number of passengers we'll be carrying, I can't promise anything until we get to the Ohio."

The North Star stopped at Burning Springs only long enough to take on passengers. They chugged on up the Kanawha at what seemed to Amber a crawl. Thankfully she slept much of the time. When she awoke she spent every second in prayer, not only for safety but for the alleviation of leg cramps. She tried to pray for her Mama, also, but that brought on tears so she decided not to think about it.

One of the passengers confided to Captain Phil that he was travelling to Gallipolis to check on a legal matter with Judge Marcus Woodcutter.

"Are you certain he will be home?" asked the Captain guardedly. "He travels much of the time to Federal courts."

"He'd better be there. He wrote me to come this very day to consult with him on this."

"Hmm. Well, then, I'm sure you can count on it. From what I hear the Judge is a man of his word. Er, excuse me, sir. I need to go relieve the man at the wheel. We need to swing just a bit east in the Ohio to deliver this keg of whiskey afore we head west into the town.''

He pulled the North Star up at the end of the walk up to where the Stivers lived. Thankful that Amber was such a petite little thing, he hoisted the whiskey keg up to his shoulder.

"Have a quick delivery to make up this hill, folks. Sorry for the delay. But we'll still be docking at Gallipolis ahead of schedule." This was said over his shoulder as he trotted up the hill.

He kicked at the door, awakening Hannah from a nap. "Here's your whiskey, Mistress Stivers," he exclaimed, thinking how sometimes in this business even the woods had ears.

Hannah stood aghast as he entered the room and put the barrel down. Deftly removing the lid, he lifted the frightened child out of the keg.

"Miss Hannah, meet Amber, your first traveller. And, Amber, this child who can't seem to close her mouth is Prudy. I think the two of you are probably of an age."

"I'm sorry," he explained to Hannah, "but I must press on. The North Star is full of passengers. And some of them have paid their fare beyond Gallipolis. I can't get back afore day after tomorrow. Just keep her out of sight whatever you do. Someone will contact you tonight about her. Be careful!"

Before Hannah had even taken a breath, he was gone. "Would you like to sit down, Miss Amber?" she asked.

"Oh, no, please Ma'am. I's been in that barrel for the longest time. But could I have a drink of water?" As she spoke, she walked around the room, stretching and flexing every muscle in her body. After gulping the entire dipper of water, she glanced all around her. "Is I free yet? Miss Libby said that once I got into Ohio, I'd be free. Is this Ohio?"

Hannah hugged the child. "Well, yes, you are in Ohio. And, of a truth, you are free. But we've still got to be real careful about bounty hunters and such. In a few more days of travelling, you'll be completely free. So you met Libby, did you? She's my daughter."

Prudy joined in the conversation and before long the three of them were chatting away like old friends. They made plans to conceal Amber in the cellar if necessary, and Prudy led her through the secret passageway to the springhouse just for practice. Then they closed the curtains at all the windows and left the cellar door ajar.

In town, one of the passengers on the North Star stopped in at Le Clerque's Mercantile before making his way to the family he was visiting.

The store owner asked hopefully, "Een what way may I be of service to you, Monsieur?"

"Tell me where a man can buy whiskey in this town. I'd like to take a keg with me to the man I'll be staying with. I wanted to buy some off the boat captain, but he delivered the only keg he had to the widow who lives just east of the Kanawha."

Le Clerque's eyes narrowed. "He deed, deed he? Hmm. Very interesting. Well, as to the whiskey, try one of the taverns. I'm just on my way to 'Our House.' Come. I weel show you the way."

Late that night there was the unmistakable sound of hoofbeats coming into Hannah's yard. "Girls, to the cellar!'' she instructed. ''Prudy, you listen carefully. You'll know if it is safe to come up.''

She dropped the door to the cellar just as a knock sounded on her door.

''Just a moment,'' she called as she spread the rag rug over the trap door and pulled her wooden rocker over the rug. With a final reassuring glance at the concealed cellar opening, she went to the door.

''Who is it?''

''Open up, lady. I's got search warrants of every kind.''

Hannah opened the door a crack, but planted her body in the opening. Gripping the doorjamb to support her suddenly trembling body, she tried to appear calm.

''Search warrants? Why, whatever for? And who are you anyway?''

''Name's Lucius, if it's any of your business. And we're lookin' fer a little nigger gal. We've got reason to believe she's here. What say you let me in?''

''Why, sir, I'm not accustomed to allowing strange men to enter my . . .''

At this point the hateful Lucius shoved the door open. Hannah nearly fell. As she righted herself, she saw that there was a group of men with him. Four that she could see, and who knew how many others?

Stumbling to the rocking chair, she spoke in a loud voice, clearly enunciating each syllable.

''Just go ahead then, men. I've nothing whatsoever to hide. I certainly haven't seen any slave girl.'' She reasoned in her heart that this was not a lie, for Amber was now free. She rocked slowly and casually as the men stormed through her things.

"Hmm. Looky here, Lucius! Ain't this what the Frenchman meant?" said a big, dark-complexioned man as he pointed to the empty whisky keg.

"Supposin' you tell us what was in this here keg. And we know you jest got it delivered today. So don't go tryin' no funny business. It's obvious that you ain't drunk no keg of whiskey today!"

"Why didn't I think of the keg?" Hannah wondered. Silently she prayed, "Lord, let Prudy get her through the tunnel and on to safety." Aloud she said, "I don't know what you men mean. Isn't it obvious that there's no slave girl here?"

Trained in the school of Miss Constance Woodcutter, Prudence proved herself an able conductor on the Underground Railroad. As soon as she heard the ruckus overhead, she swung aside the sliding shelves and she and Amber were on their way. She crouched low at a bush beside the springhouse and stared back at her Cowma's house. She hated to leave while the men were still there harassing Cowma, but she knew it was what she would be expected to do.

"Lord, lead her," she whispered. Taking Amber's hand, she ran through the woods she knew like the back of her hand.

Though the men would continue their search for days, Amber was never seen in that area again. Her quest for freedom finally was realized when she stepped on Canadian soil a week later.

Lucius had never been more exasperated. This search had been long and hard and still he had nothing to show for all his long hours in the saddle.

"Maybe she ain't here now, Boss, but she surely and

purely was here. Of that I feel certain," said one of his cohorts as they mounted up.

"It's time these lousy abolitionists learnt a lesson," said the hateful overseer. "Burn it!" he commanded.

Rebel yells filled the air as the men circled Hannah's house and threw flaming torches on the roof.

A great peace settled on Hannah. She heard the goings on. She smelled the smoke but she must keep rocking to give the girls every second they needed to escape. There was plenty of time for her to make her way to the door and safety. The room began to fill with smoke. The fire burned through the ceiling in two places. Cinders began to fall all around Hannah.

"They're surely clear by now," she thought and, beginning to cough, she groped toward the door. Just as she reached it, the framing collapsed and the crosspiece hit her square in the temple. She fell out the doorway with a dull thud.

The cowardly men, now frightened by their actions, never slowed their horses till they reached the edge of Gallipolis.

Before the fire got a real good start, the heavens opened with a great downpour and a wind kicked up from the east which blew the smoke and debris all away from the porch where Hannah lay. Willy and Nancy returned the next afternoon to find a dazed Prudy sitting in the ashes with her beloved Cowma's head cradled in her lap.

❊　❊　❊　❊　❊

Hannah awoke in a field of clover beside a beautiful

river. Or was she dreaming? She hadn't seen flowers this beautiful since she and Will left Germany. The colors were so vivid. The reds were so bright and the yellows so yellow! The sky overhead was so blue she shielded her eyes. Yet there was no sun shining.

"This must be a dream," she told herself again. "This river . . . I don't think it is the Ohio. There's a man over there. I'll call to him and find out where I am. Why, he looks like . . . oh, now I know it's a dream!"

The man had turned to face her. She remembered every detail of that face. He broke into a beautiful smile. The beloved dimple was still in his chin.

"Hannah," he whispered. Though he was far away, she could hear it distinctly. "Come on over," he motioned. "The river looks dark and foreboding, but it's not as bad as it seems. Come, Hannah. Hurry!"

She ran toward the river. Could it possibly be? But his shoulders were no longer hunched over. He stood so straight and tall.

As her feet began to splash in the current, she felt tears on her face. "Will? My darling, can it really be you?"

Her feet were as nimble as they'd been so many years before when she'd met him in a garden in Germany. By the time she reached the opposite shore, her tears were dry. "Will?" she kept repeating. "Will?"

And then they stood hand in hand, her blue eyes staring up into his black ones. "Is Duffy here? And the babies? Oh, Will, is it really you?"

Pulling her into his arms at last, he whispered, "Oh, yes, Hannah. They're here. And yes, it's really me. Hannah, darling, I've waited for you for so very long.

Welcome home, my lady!''